MW00876088

ANTHONY
&
CATHERINE

WILLOW WINTERS
WALL STREET JOURNAL & USA TODAY BESTSELLING AUTHOR

From USA Today bestselling author Willow Winters comes a HOT mafia, standalone romance.

I'm a dangerous man. You may be fooled by my good looks and charm, but my eyes give it away.

I'm the hitman for the Valetti familia, and I'm damn good at what I do.

They want men to talk, and I make them talk. They want men gone — bang, it's done. It's as simple as that.

Until her.
She's on my list, but I want her. On her knees and submitting to my every command.
I'll give her a simple choice — die, or be mine.

I've always wanted this.
Now that I have the chance, I'm taking it.

I can fulfill those fantasies I know she has.
'm going to make her beg for it.

BAD
BOY

CHAPTER 1

ANTHONY

I stare at the picture from the envelope and feel so damn conflicted. I crumple the edges in my hand, not knowing if I really wanna go through with this. My eyes travel along each feature of her face, pausing to admire her large, brown eyes and long, thick lashes. She has gorgeous full lips I want to bite, but also see wrapped around my cock. Her nails are done in a classic shade of red, and her light brown hair hangs over her shoulders in loose curls. Her breasts peek out just above the neckline of her flowing blouse. I wish I could slowly strip her out of those clothes. But I can't. She's not mine. Even worse, I'm supposed to kill her.

I shove the slip of paper back into the envelope containing

the other photos, those hits I couldn't give two shits about. They're for assholes who have it coming to them. One stole and ran in order to keep up with his addiction. You don't steal from a mob boss and think you can get away with it. The second killed a made man. He knows it's coming. Neither are doing a good job of hiding. They'll be easy hits.

I take another swig from my beer and debate on taking the sheet back out. But I have her face memorized already. I want her. More than that, I want to break her. My thoughts are depraved, and I know it. I think back to the last chick I had. She liked to play. But that's all it was to her. Play. I want the real thing. I want to earn a woman's submission, earn her desire to please me through training. So far, it's always been pretend. I've never had an opportunity like this. But it's wrong. It's so fucked up and wrong.

But then again, so am I.

I carve up assholes and kill them for a living. The torturing and their screams don't affect me in the least.

This broad has it coming to her, even if she doesn't know it. She probably thought she was doing the right thing by going to the cops. She probably thinks she's safe in the witness protection program. She's not. She didn't know what she was doing, and now it's my responsibility to make her disappear. She cost the Cassano *familia* a lot of money, but more than anything, they lost face. The fucker she was involved with doesn't care that she's on a hit list. He's just pissed she ratted on them, even if the charges didn't stick.

Killing her is purely about their pride and the deal they lost.

I grind my teeth and slowly peel back the label on my beer bottle. I have to be delicate so it doesn't tear apart. Patience. I need patience. With everything I do, I need patience.

I've been looking into her, and I know she'd fit the part. Poor girl didn't know what she was getting herself into when she started fucking around with a member of the Cassanos. She's a sweet little thing who thought she'd like a taste of the more dangerous things in life. I can give her more than a taste though. I can give her exactly what she was looking for and fulfill those fantasies I know she has. And she can give me what I've always wanted.

I spied on her again last night. She was reading one of her books, and I watched as it turned her on. Of course she had no idea, but I was right fucking there. The only thing separating us was a brick wall. With her window open, I clearly heard all those soft moans coming from her lips. I had to know what she was reading, so I sneaked in and took a look around.

I Googled that book the second I got home. Her own dark desires sealed her fate.

She has deviant fantasies just like me. She's fucking perfect.

"Anthony, you wanna talk now?" I hear Vince ask as he pulls up the stool to my right. I messaged him earlier. I place my bottle on the bar and push it to one side as the bartender slides Vince his usual Jack.

I lean back a bit and tap my knuckles on the bar before facing him. Vince is a ruthless fucker, and he doesn't take any shit. He's also my cousin, so I feel safe with him. But this is the mob, and he's the Don. I'm never *that* safe.

"It's about the hits we got in," I tell him in a low enough voice that no one else present is going to hear. Not that it matters. It's our bar, and we know everyone in here.

"You need help? Tommy's not enough?" he asks, cocking a brow. Tommy's my brother, and he's also my second-in-command. Technically we're both contractors for the *familia*. We only do hits, and we don't bother with that other bullshit.

"No," I say with certitude. I never need help. Hits are easy for me, in addition to being good money.

He takes a sip and licks his lips. "What's the problem, then?" he asks.

"There's one that I'd rather not do," I tell him.

"Why's that?" he asks, setting the glass down to face me with his shoulders squared. He's in business mode. Right now he's not a friend, and he's not my cousin. Right now he's the boss.

"I want to make them an offer instead," I explain.

His brow furrows as he replies. "I'm listening."

"One's a woman." His eyes flash with sympathy. None of us like taking women out. It's something that rarely happens, but when it does, we don't like it. We make it quick and painless for them. Maybe it's sexist, but I don't give a fuck.

I've tortured a lot of men for information. Never a woman though. That's where I draw the line.

"They won't let her walk." His words are said with finality.

"I want to ask if they'd accept a substantial monetary offer from me to buy her." I feel my blood rushing faster and hotter. No one knows about my perversions. I'm sure they can all guess. But I've never said a thing about my tastes, and they've never asked. They keep me on the edge of the social circle for the most part. I'm fine with that. It's better that way.

"Buy her, and then what?" he asks with his eyes trained on the back of the bar.

"I want to keep her." My voice is low, but steady.

"As a pet? As a slave?" Equal amounts of disgust and disbelief color his voice, and it almost makes me regret letting my dark desire come to light. Almost. But I want this. I want it more than anything.

"If that's what you want to call it." The determination in my voice rings out clearly. I'm sure my eyes look dark and absolute. I'm not ashamed of what I want. But I'm not willing to risk my position in the *familia* over it. Not yet, anyway. It's been a week since I was given the hit. Each day my obsession with her has only grown. I cleared out a room for her already. In my head, she's already mine. This is just a formality. But to Vince, this is a twisted sickness.

He looks me dead in the eyes as he begins, "After that shit Ava went through--"

I stop him right there and say, "This would be nothing like that." My voice is louder than it should be, and the dark stare he gives me in return makes that clear. I settle in my seat and continue with a respectful tone. "I would never hurt her. Not like that. Not beyond any pain she didn't want."

"Ava said some days she would've rather been dead than been in that position." My heart hurts for her. Ava's a *comare* to a member of our *familia*. To Kane. He's a good man. He saved her, and in a lot of ways, she saved him as well.

She went through a lot of shit. Her captors loved hurting her and humiliating her. She's a strong woman to have survived all that. That's not what I want though. The idea of doing that to a woman makes me angry. I'd never do that. Never.

"It's not the same." I reach for my beer and turn away from him slightly. He doesn't understand. I didn't expect him to anyway. "She's already dead. She's on their list." I take a drink and then look back to him. "I'll give her a choice."

"Death, or your slave?" he asks with a humorless grunt. I know to him she'd be seen as a slave, as a pet. That's fine. To me, she'd be *mine*. Nothing else but mine.

"Better than death with no escape," I respond flatly.

He takes a sip of Jack, looks at me, and says, "It may not be to her. You want to hurt her and abuse her, rather than carrying out an order that would give her a quick death."

"No. I don't want that. It's not like that." He doesn't fucking get it. I torture and kill people for a living. I can see how he thinks that's what I'd do to her. But I wouldn't. I don't know how much I should explain. To be honest, I don't fucking feel like explaining anything.

My blood heats with anger, but then I have a pang of worry and think, *What if she doesn't get it either?* I brush my doubt aside. I'll show her. I'll have to teach her how perfect it would be to be mine. I've looked into her. I've been obsessed with learning everything about her. She's smart. She'll learn. She'll catch on quick that I'll be a good master to her. And she's familiar with the concepts. She's read enough to have an idea of what I want from her. "Think of it as hardcore BDSM," I say. I look at him from the corner of my eye, but it's not convincing him.

I want this too fucking badly to let this opportunity pass me by. And after thinking about all the ways she'd calm the beast in me, I don't know if I could actually go through with killing her.

Vince shakes his head and asks, "What are you looking to get from me, Anthony?"

"I want your permission to offer them a deal for her." I need my proposal presented to the Cassano boss. He's the one who ordered the hit. A number of other bosses come to us for hits, and we take care of their messes. For the right price, anyway. I don't want to piss anyone off, and I want this to be a clean deal. Vince is quiet for a long time as he considers.

"You won't hurt her?" he finally asks.

"I won't. It's about something else for me." Control. Desire. Submission. I want it all from her, but not her pain.

He nods his head once and I take that as an agreement. I can't help that an asymmetric smile grows on my face. Step one is done. Now to contact the other mob head. He'll be easy to convince, I'm sure. He didn't give a fuck about the soldiers she gave up. He cares about the deal he lost, and the money that went with it.

I down the rest of my beer and nod a goodbye to Vince. I don't have anything else to say to him. I'd rather he forget this conversation ever happened.

As I turn to leave, eager to clear out the cell I've prepared for her and put the finishing touches in her room, he turns in his seat and grabs my arm to stop me.

"What are you going to do if she chooses death?" he asks as I turn to face him. The idea of her dying makes my heart stop in my chest.

"I'll make sure that doesn't happen." Chills run down my body at the thought of those beautiful eyes staring into mine, begging me for death. That's not what I want. I know she'll want this when I show her how good it can be.

"It might," he says, looking at me with sympathy in his eyes. I don't want his sympathy.

She's going to fucking love what I do to her. But I'll have to break her first.

CHAPTER 2

CATHERINE
THREE WEEKS LATER

I tip the edge of the porcelain cup to my lips and close my eyes as the perfect temperature of tea spills into my mouth. My eyes close and the comfort of routine washes through me. But the feeling is only temporary. That's when I register the change. Something feels off. I remember thinking that earlier as well. It's too quiet. Crickets and other creatures of the night always provide soothing background noise for my evening tea. But tonight the noises are muted. It's as though something's scared them away.

I always drink chamomile tea to help me relax and sleep. My normal routine is to sit on the porch while I finish a cup, followed by a melatonin pill. I've had issues falling to sleep for the last year or so. Ever since my life completely changed. Staying asleep is never an issue, but falling asleep is difficult. In the year that I've been here, I've done the same thing every night.

Before my life changed forever, I didn't have a care in the world and slept like a baby every night. I did whatever I wanted, whenever I wanted. Then I hit my mid-twenties and decided I needed to sow my wild oats. My mother had just passed away. She was older when she had me, and she died peacefully--as peacefully as you can with cancer--but it was hard on me and I didn't want to face the pain. To say I engaged in high-risk behavior would be putting it lightly. Then I fell in love. Or rather, what I *thought* was love with an asshole named Lorenzo Passanova. I called him my Cassanova because I was a fucking idiot, high on lust and loving the risk that came with being with a man like him.

I thought being with him would be just like the books I love to read. Like I'd be living out the plot of a romance novel. I was a fucking idiot.

Meeting that asshole was the worst thing that ever happened to me. I didn't even realize it until it was too late. He sucked me out of my safe little bubble into his world, and I felt alive for the first time in my life. But it was a mistake. A horrible fucking mistake.

When you play with fire, expect to get burned. Over and over, I'd heard my mother's warning, but I ignored it. The first time it happened, I knew I'd seriously misjudged him.

Lorenzo smacked me so hard across the face that I fell to the ground. Even worse, I eventually tried to sneak out and leave his ass behind, but ran into his *familia* beating the shit out of a guy. Bags of dope were scattered everywhere as they made their threats. That was it for me. I saw and heard too much. I ran like hell, but they got me. They cornered me and took me back to Lorenzo and then to their Don.

Lorenzo beat the hell out of me in front of them. He told them he'd keep me in line for now, so they didn't have to kill me right then. His *familia* were cold-blooded murderers who wanted me dead. I'll never forget the looks in their eyes. Or the disgusting joy that filled Lorenzo's dark eyes when he would repeatedly hurt me. I had one chance to slip away, and I took it. I ran like hell and blabbed to the police so they'd protect me.

That's what living on the edge got me. As a result, I've settled my ass down tremendously. And now I'm back to being the good girl my mother raised me to be. Being through that shit and getting placed in the witness protection plan will do that to you.

So now I stay in my cozy house feeling alone but safe, and surround myself with comfort and familiarity. It's different now; I'm more alone than I've ever been in my entire life, but at least I'm safe. The last time the marshals checked in on me was nearly three months ago. Now I'm on my own and settled in.

This screened-in porch is now my favorite room in this

snug, raised ranch house.

My toes sweep across the soft and high pile of the rug beneath the wicker furniture set. Across from me I have my antique curio cabinet. It contains my large collection of teapots and cups. When I run a load of laundry, I can faintly smell it from here. I inhale deeply and my lungs fill with all my favorite scents.

But the best part is the location. I'm nearly half a mile away from anyone. My home is set back into the woods and I'm surrounded by trees. The moonlight shines down and tonight it's full, illuminating the woods as though it's nearly dawn. Usually my ritual helps put me at ease, but tonight it's less familiar, less comforting.

The night air feels a bit colder on my shoulders, sending a shiver down my back. I wrap the cashmere throw tighter around myself, all the way up to my neck. I feel my forehead crease as I realize I feel someone's eyes on me. The sensation freezes my body for a moment as the fear I had nearly every night when I first moved here returns. I turn quickly in my seat and feel my heart racing. The sound of blood rushing through my ears is all I can hear. When I first moved here, I was terrified the Cassanos would find me. But they didn't. It took a long time for me to feel safe, and an even longer time for the nightmares to stop, but it's all over now. I breathe in deep and concentrate on relaxing.

I settle my back against the seat, thinking I'm just being

paranoid. A thought occurs to me. *Maybe this is my survival instinct warning me.* The idea causes a row of goosebumps to travel down my arms. But just like all of the anxiety I've dealt with this week, I push it down and chalk it up to my nerves.

I place the teacup down gently on the table and stand up, stretching slightly and covering my mouth as I yawn. The blanket slips off my shoulders, and a chill runs through my body. I'm quick to pull it back up to cover me and grip it close. Fall must be coming. It's the change of the season that's throwing me off. I close my eyes and listen harder. Some noises are faint, but they're still present. I just need to relax and accept the approaching transition from summer to autumn. Some things can't be helped.

Still, I check the locks at the front door twice after depositing my cup in the sink. Being alone in a cabin in the country isn't the smartest thing for a young woman on her own. My options for disappearing and starting a new life were limited though, and when you want to hide, it's best to be far away and alone.

I move the curtain away from the large window in the front room and look down the gravel driveway, seeing nothing. The grass is tall and needs to be mowed. I sigh and again the throw slips, but it's warmer inside the main part of the house, so I let it drape over the crook in my arm.

My bed is made and I can't wait to sink into it and drift to sleep, but I need to check over my email and messages one last time before I can pass out. The one good thing about my job is that I can do it from anywhere. When I first moved here, I had to stop working on anything associated with my real name. My blog, my columns and articles, anything else tied to my online presence, you name it—done. I was crushed. I had been a renowned book reviewer, beta reader, and part-time writer. The money was great, but I would have loved it all regardless of the pay.

I had to say goodbye to my former life though because the Cassano *familia* could have found me that way. The mafia that saw me as a rat could have easily tracked me down if I'd continued working under my real name, and it wasn't worth it.

So I started over under a pen name, and it's going better than I ever imagined it could. The experience and knowledge that I gained in my former life helped me tremendously. Now I'm firmly established in the industry, and I'm doing even better than I was before.

This is my life now--books and tea in a remote cabin in the woods. I love it, but lately it's felt empty. I could go on like this, feeling as though I'm living a full life, but I'm so alone. I wanted nothing more than to be by myself when I was running and hiding. But now I find myself questioning if I'll ever have anyone real in my life, and anything substantial.

I've thought about getting a dog—a big one, to help make me feel secure. A dog's love is unconditional. I want that love desperately. I need it from someone, or something. But a dog would need walks and interaction, and plus dogs have to be taken to the vet. Those are all opportunities for people to see me. I don't want that. I want to stay hidden. I *need* to stay hidden. But I do need companionship. I've been craving it more and more as I've settled into this new life.

At least I have my business. I have my blogging, my books, and my friends, even if they're all online. I almost didn't start over. I almost gave up and poured my heart into a book of my own. But my life is no romance. And writing it down would make it real. Once I'd gotten over the fear, I didn't want to relive it. So I did my best to move on.

I was hesitant to start from scratch, but I pushed myself to do it anyway. Within two months my new blog had taken off, and I'd revitalized my income. I log on and see twelve new messages in my email. The first few are easy enough to reply to, requiring nothing more than copying and pasting from a template of other answers I've already given. The next email takes some time to write out though. I'm responding to a new author who messaged me looking for advice on her series. I'll have to get back to her in the morning. I don't have the energy right now. But I take this business seriously, and it shows. And it pays. Just before I close the laptop, I hear a *ping*.

It's a message from a new book friend. She joined my book club a few weeks ago. Right now it's just a small Facebook group, but it's my baby. Although she's not very active in the group, she's messaged me a number of times. I get so many messages a day. Some are from other bloggers and columnists who are just starting out and looking for advice. Others are from authors wanting to send me advanced reading copies and beta reads. I can read two books a day, so I'm always happy to help where I can. But Val's messages are different. They're more personal.

What did you think of the book?

I scan the message twice as my fingers hover above the keys. I read and receive so many books that most of the time I have to sift through my emails before replying in order to make sure I'm keeping everything straight, but not this time. I know exactly which book Val's referring to.

Smut, also known as erotic romance to some, is a genre with which I'm intimately familiar. I prefer the term smut though, because it fills me with life. Like I'm naughty for reading it. The book she picked out though is exceptionally taboo. Arousal heats my core. The idea of being taken by a strange man has certainly been a dark desire of my own. I clench my thighs and bite down on my lip. I won't admit how I touched myself to some scenes.

I decide to respond with a professional answer.

I thought the author did a fabulous job of depicting the scenes with vivid imagery and capturing the heroine's emotions and character arc. Overall a well-written book.

She's quick with a reply. *So you enjoyed it?*

I did, I message back.

Is it so wrong that I'd want it to come true? Her reply makes me stop and consider her words.

I don't think there's anything wrong with the fantasy. But I'm sure real life would be much different.

You don't think you'd enjoy it in real life? Her question forces a small laugh from my lips. Although it's wonderful to get lost in them, these books aren't real. I know I'd enjoy some things. I've often fantasized about them. But this conversation is veering a little more into the territory of my personal preferences and is less about the book. It's also late, and I need to go to sleep while the melatonin is still active or I'll never get to bed. So I settle for a quick reply with a little humor that she'd enjoy.

Oh there are scenes I'd enjoy, but I'll stick to role playing for that ;) Gotta go to bed, ttyl!

Night!

A shiver of want travels through me as I exit her message and look at the list of remaining emails. I'll get to them all tomorrow.

I close my laptop, but I feel more awake now than I was when I first sat down. The book Val mentioned is all I can think about as I change into a nightgown. The imagery of a dark, damp cell and chains flood my mind. I can picture being the heroine. I can understand her desire to please her master. I wasn't a huge fan of the ending though. It wasn't the happily ever after I enjoy from romance. It was more realistic. After all, how could you ever fall in love with your captor, but still be sane? Would it even be possible to have both the sweet fantasy and the dark reality?

As I crawl into bed and lie on my back, I let my fingertips gently brush along my clit as I think about the book. I hear the clinking of the chains and the smack of the whip. I see her back arch as she raises her lower half to him for more. He takes her however he wants, and she's more than happy to let him use her body. My legs part, and I dip my fingers into my slick pussy and run the moisture over my clit. A small moan escapes me as I see the scenes play out in my head.

She's been trained to love the sting of the belt, and the feel of his hand slapping her ass. His bites. His marks. My hand grips my breast and I pinch my nipple between my fingers and pull, imagining it's him. I turn my head as though his lips are touching my neck, as if his teeth are about to pierce my skin. Anything and everything he does to her is a reward. He thrusts into her and takes his pleasure, over and over. Using her body. And she enjoys it. She thrives under his touch. I circle my clit, wanting him to reward her for her obedience. It's all she lives for. She is his, and that's all she desires. She only lives to please him. He doesn't stop until he has his fill and cums deep inside her. That alone is enough to bring her over the edge. And I find my own release with her.

You don't think you'd enjoy it in real life?

I remember Val's question as my breath steadies and I

turn on my side, feeling exhausted from cumming.

In real life, that scenario would be a fucking nightmare. Just as I close my eyes, I feel a pinch in my neck. My lips part as I wince and raise my hand to feel what caused the sting, but it falls lifeless to my side. I vaguely make out a dark figure rounding the bed to approach me.

"Sleep, kitten." I hear his voice. But I can't respond as darkness overwhelms me.

CHAPTER 3

CATHERINE

My shoulders are so sore. I roll onto my back against the cold, hard concrete and wince. After taking a moment to adjust to the discomfort, I push off the floor and into a sitting position. My eyes open and try to adapt to the darkness. I can barely see anything. My heart pounds in my chest, beating faster than it ever has before. I have no idea where I am or how I got here, but this shit isn't good. A cold sweat pricks my skin as I think back to last night. I remember lying down in my bed. I was tired, and then I fell asleep.

I have no clue how I've ended up here, in the middle of what looks like a small basement cellar. It's nearly pitch black. The only light is streaming through three small windows high up on the ceiling of the far wall. Each window is only about the size of a cinder block, and all three are blocked by something, but a small bit of light is still shining through. Terror runs through me and seems to freeze my blood.

I open my mouth to scream, but I'm too scared. *They'll* hear me.

I've been taken. They found me, and they took me. I know exactly who it is. The Cassanos. Fuck! I never want to go back to him, to Lorenzo. I won't let him touch me ever again.

Tears threaten to reveal themselves. But it's useless to cry. Some small part of me always knew it would come to this. You can't escape your death. I didn't really think I'd ever be able to run. I swallow the lump growing in my throat. My eyes fall to the ground. I have no idea why they would keep me alive, since I'm no use to them. I'm certain they'll kill me soon. Or worse.

There are only two options I can think of. One, they left me alive to torture me because I went to the cops. Two, they left me alive to torture me for fun. Knowing Lorenzo, it's number two.

I close my eyes, letting the realization settle in. My body shakes as tremors of fear run through my limbs, but I try to soothe them. I got out before. I'll do it again. I may be a meek little mouse, as that fucker used to call me, but I fight when I have to. And right now, I have to.

My eyes slowly open and adjust to the light.

The air is cold and damp, but my throw is in a pile on

the floor next to me. I quickly grab it and wrap it around me as though it can protect me. Fear cripples me as I hear the sound of a chair moving across the floor. My heart stills and a chill prickles my skin. I'm not alone.

As I search the dark, vacant room, I see him. The look of a hunter stares back at me. I don't recognize him. His broad chest and chiseled muscles flex as he leans forward. His eyes are a brilliant light blue and they pierce through me. His cheekbones are sharp and only appear more contoured with the shadows from the dim light. If he had any other expression on his face, I'd think he was the most gorgeous man I've ever met.

As if reading my mind, he smirks at me. The fucking bastard thinks this is funny. My heart tries to climb up my throat as he sits back in his seat and his hand settles on the raging erection in his jeans.

Fuck!

My eyes dart back up to his. That shit's not happening. I'll claw his fucking eyes out. I look for a door and then back to him. I don't see one, but I don't care if I kill him and I'm locked in here and starve to death. I won't let that happen.

We stare at each other in silence. I want to ask him what he wants from me, but I already know. I want to plead for him to let me leave, but I've learned that doesn't work. Instead I wait for his move. He cocks his head after a moment and slowly stands.

As he moves toward me, I resist the urge to scoot away. I

can't do that. I can't back myself into a corner.

He crouches in front of me and leans in closer. His eyes hold a hint of danger, but also a spark of desire. I'm just not sure what he wants to do with me exactly, besides the obvious. "I'm supposed to kill you," he says. His deep baritone voice is low and threatening. He tilts his head as I slide slightly backward on my ass out of natural instinct. I take control of my body and tilt my chest away from him, giving myself leverage to kick this motherfucker in the balls if he gets any closer.

His full lips pull into an asymmetric grin. "You can't get away from me just yet." I hate how he's taunting me, like he expected this.

My breathing is ragged, and my heart is beating so fast I swear my chest won't be able to contain it. It feels as though my heart's trying to leap out of my throat. I barely get the words out, but I manage to say, "I don't want to die."

His grin widens into a perfect smile. This man's too handsome to be a predator. There's a darkness about him, but he could fool anyone with just a small amount of charm.

"I don't want you to die either, kitten." His pet name sends a bolt of desire to my clit. Shame washes through me. I shouldn't like it. *This is wrong.* He stands up and towers above me. I tilt my head to keep my eyes on him. "You have a choice," he says.

I wait for him to continue as I stay huddled in a ball beneath him. My blood rushes loudly in my ears and I try to calm my racing heart. He doesn't want me to die. That should relax me; it should make me feel even the faintest bit better. But it doesn't.

"You can die." He speaks to the far wall, not looking at me. I find my eyes searching for a door, looking for a way out. To my right, I finally spot a steel door, with a keypad to its left. "Or," he continues, and I feel his gaze on me as my eyes fly to meet his and my heart thuds painfully in my chest. "You can agree to be *mine*."

I can't help that the way he says it makes my core heat. A wetness pools between my thighs and I feel ashamed. This isn't a fantasy. This is real life. I feel the blood drain from my face as I become lightheaded. The only reason I'm not dead is because he wants to keep me. But I doubt his intentions are anything but kinky and sick.

I don't want this. Tears leak from the corners of my eyes and I shake my head. "No." My voice is hoarse and barely audible.

This isn't real. This isn't happening. I wait for him to grab me. As soon as he does, I'll strike. But he merely searches my face for something and stands far enough away that I can't do any real damage.

He cocks a brow and his voice softens as he says, "You haven't heard my terms. How sure are you that you don't want to be my pet?"

Terms?

Again the offer makes my pussy clench and my cheeks

redden with a violent blush. "No," I blurt out without thinking.

His chest rumbles with a deep chuckle. "Some part of you wants me. There's hope for us after all." He smiles down at me and turns to walk away. My limbs refuse to move and attack him. Instead I stay frozen on the ground. I watch his corded muscles ripple as he walks to the door and enters in a code.

"Where are you going?" I ask before thinking. Apparently the fear of being left alone in this room to rot is greater than my fear of him. I don't want to die here, left to starve because he changed his mind. I may have said no, but I sure as fuck don't want to die here.

He turns and gives me the same sexy smirk. "My kitten needs to eat."

Tension coils in my body. I can't let him leave. I need to get more information. I don't like not knowing anything about this situation and not having any other options.

"Wait. What--" I swallow thickly before continuing. "What are your terms?"

He smirks at me as he opens the door and says, "The first is that you'll listen to me. I'll be back soon."

My chest rises and falls with anxiety and fear as I stare back at him in silence. I pull the throw tighter around my shoulders and watch as he walks through the door and leaves me in the dark room. I'm all alone and barely able to breathe. After a short moment, lights in the ceiling slowly come to life, illuminating the room dimly and gradually getting brighter.

I look around my surroundings and see a small toilet in the corner and the metal chair my captor was sitting in, but nothing else. Tears prick my eyes and my blood runs cold. I can't stay here like a prisoner.

I stare at the door waiting for him to come back, letting everything sink in.

I've been taken.

And he wants to keep me.

The only thing I'm certain of is that I need to find a way out of here. Run as fast as I can, and never look back. But I'll have to rely on him to get out of this fucking cell first.

CHAPTER 4

ANTHONY

I've never done anything that's felt this *wrong* before. Nothing's ever come close to giving me this thrill that's surging in my blood. Her reaction was perfect. I knew she'd deny me, but the fight in her is something I didn't expect. I fucking love it.

I had to be in there when she woke up. I didn't want her freaking out, thinking she was going to die. Instead she can be absorbed with thoughts of me and being mine. My dick is fucking leaking in my jeans. I can't help that I want this. I want her. And now I have her. But not her submission though. That much is obvious and expected.

I feel like I'm on the highest high I've ever had in my life.

I should feel conflicted. I should have second thoughts about this, or feel remorse. But I don't. *She's mine.*

I pace back and forth in the kitchen as I think about what I'd like to feed her. I'm not sure what to offer her first. I need to make it tempting for her to obey me, but this isn't a reward. I have to stay vigilant. I want to shower her with everything she'd ever want to convince her she'd enjoy being my pet. But that would defeat the entire purpose of all this, and she needs to know what her position is. She needs to earn her rewards just as much as I need to earn her submission.

There are simple truths to this relationship.

I will always give her shelter and food, no matter how disobedient she is. Even if she refuses every order, which I imagine will happen at some point. Hell, I fully expect her to try to kill me at some point, too. Even the best submissives refuse their positions at times. And she's being forced into this, so I wouldn't blame her if she did. There's no reason for me to deliver physical punishment unless I'd like to prep her for pleasure. Which I can't fucking wait to do.

I imagine it'll be her mouth that makes me blister her ass red. My dick jumps in my pants at the thought of watching her ass turn a beautiful shade as my palm smacks against her pale skin.

Equally as important as punishment is reward.

Although I'll always feed her, some kinds of food are definitely a reward. This won't be one of them. But it needs to be good. She didn't eat dinner, so I know she must be hungry. It's far past breakfast, so a light brunch it is.

I looked up her credit card history and I know what she likes to eat. I've taken everything she does into consideration. I know everything about her. I've spent every day for nearly a month studying her habits and learning how best I can meet her needs and reward her. I also needed time to get the rooms together and decide on the best way to go about everything in between taking care of the other hits. I've fantasized about this day since I got the approval from the mob bosses. But I never imagined I'd get this fucking rush of adrenaline.

One thing I hadn't decided was what her first meal should be.

Although she's not too picky, I don't want it to be mediocre. However, I can't spoil her just yet, so I decide on fresh ahi tuna. It's something that will be simple to feed her. I smile as I realize I'm going to feed my kitten tuna. A rough chuckle rumbles through my chest. I'm sure she won't find humor in that, but I sure as fuck do.

I grab the tuna tartare from the fridge. It's fresh. I bought it just for her since it's one of her favorites. I'll give it to her now even though it's certainly on the reward side of food. She needs to know I'll treat her well and give her what she likes so long as she obeys. She'll probably throw it in my face or on the ground, but I'm prepared for that to happen. And then she'll have to settle for something less appealing when I serve her dinner.

If she's a good girl, I'll move her into her room. I don't think she'll react well to being kept and told to obey, but the thought makes my dick press even harder against my zipper. I'm dying for her to disobey me, but there's a very real possibility that it'll take a long time to convince her that she should listen to me. I can't get carried away with my excitement. I have to be patient. I have to give her every reason I can to submit to me willingly.

She will though. I'm certain of it. I know this turns her on as much as it does me. It's what sealed her fate. We both have this fantasy, and I'd be a fucking idiot to let it pass us by. That's why I watched her for so long. I needed to make sure this is really what I wanted. And it is. She's exactly who I want. Everything she does is perfect. She's a natural submissive.

I pull back the plastic wrap holding the delicately pressed chunks together, and place the stack neatly in the center of a ceramic plate. It looks delicious. I grab the accompanying plastic container of sauce and put it on the dish. She'll enjoy this...if she eats it. I thought about using a plastic plate, but I want the dish to be breakable. I want her to think about smashing it and using it against me. Fuck, in all honesty, I hope she tries. That way I can show her how useless her struggle would be. It feeds into my need to train her to be submissive to me. Maybe it's wrong of me to tease her like that and to dare her to disobey me, but I don't give a fuck.

Right now I just need to get her to agree and follow a

simple command. To eat.

I have to adjust my erection at the thought of her parting those full lips and letting me slip chunks of tuna into her mouth. I'm so fucking hard for her. All I want to do is pin her down and sink deep into her hot cunt. I know she's turned on by this. If nothing else she wants to fuck me. It's a long way from her craving to be all mine, to wanting to submit to my every wish. But at least her desire is a start. A really good fucking start. I wasn't anticipating that just yet.

I thought she'd be crying by now. I imagined her screaming and begging to be set free. That's not what I want, but that would be a natural response. Maybe that'll come later. I'm hopeful that it won't though. She's too smart for that shit. I think she'll probably pretend to play along and wait for the perfect opportunity, just like she did earlier. She'll go along with everything, waiting to see my hand and then calculate her next move.

I'll be ready though. I can't wait till she lets her claws out and tries to fight me so I can show her just how easy it would be to take her.

I shake my head, hating where my thoughts are going. I'm such a sick fuck. For as long as I can remember, I've had these dark desires. I want her to fight me, to run from me. I want to feel her body struggle against mine. But I want her to do all of that willingly. I want her eager for me to chase her and pin her down, forcing her legs open and fucking her until she's limp and filled with my cum. I won't give in to that temptation, not until she begs me. Not until I earn it.

I can't get carried away. I need her to *want* this just as much as I do.

As I prepare to head back to her cell, my phone goes off in the dining room. From the sound I can tell it's a text, and I know it's from Vince. I put the plate on the counter and walk to the table to give him the news.

Is the shipment taken care of? he asks in his text.

Usually I'd reply with a simple yes, meaning that the unlucky bastard on my list is dead, but that's not the case this time.

It's been delivered, I respond.

You've kept the shipment?

Yes. I'm quick to answer. My heart beats faster in my chest. He gave me permission, so now I'm keeping her. I don't like that he's questioning me. Maybe he was wondering if I'd really go through with it. I watch my phone and see he's writing a response. Then nothing. Then he starts typing again. I'm not sure if he doesn't know what to say, or if he's just trying to figure out how to word it.

Will the order keep a shelf life? he asks, and I know what he's really asking. Will she live? Am I going to kill her? Or possibly he thinks she'd rather die than be with me.

I stare at my phone and look through the kitchen toward the back room where the door to the basement is. I've got all three of her rooms set up with locks on them. The cell, her suite, and her office. I didn't do all this prep work and make sure she was the one for me only to have her taken away. Or worse, have her choose death. She may have said no to being mine out of a knee-jerk reaction at first, but she's curious, and I know I can change her mind. She doesn't mean it. Before I leave her cell tonight, I'm going to leave her wanting more. I want her to start fantasizing about being mine and what an opportunity this really is for her.

I type in my answer and push send, leaving the phone on the table and walking quickly to get back to her.

I'm keeping her.

CHAPTER 5

CATHERINE

After a minute of watching the door, I slowly rise and take a look around the room. It's small and a bit cold. The only escape is the door he went through. The one locked with a keypad.

I can't fucking stay here like a caged rat. My heart stills in my chest. That's what I am to them. My eyes rise with defiance to the door. I did what I thought was right, and the only thing I could do to survive. They can all fuck off. I don't deserve this shit. I'm not a mouse or a rat.

I picture that sexy smirk and hear the man keeping me here call me *kitten*. It sends a shiver down my spine. I'm not his fucking kitten either. Even if I do think that pet name is sexy as hell, and it makes my pussy clench.

I walk to the chair and imagine smashing it against his head when that fucker gets back in here. I don't know the code to unlock the door though. I'd have to be on the other side of the room to get a good view of him punching in the keys. Even then, I doubt I'd be able to make them out; it's too fucking dark. I need to get the fuck out of this room, and I don't know how I'm going to be able to do that unless he physically lets me.

I know pleading with him to let me go would be of no use, but maybe I can beg him to let me out of this room and into another. One without a fucking lock. I need to be smart about this. I grip the back of the chair wanting so desperately to just beat the shit out of him, but I can't. First of all, I'm weak as shit. Second, no matter how much I don't like it, I'm stuck here until he decides to let me out.

My body tenses as the door opens. I watch as he walks into the room with a plate balanced in his hands. Anger heats my blood. This is a game to him. He thinks he can play with me. He stops as the door clicks shut behind him and he stares at me. I try to school my expression to neutral, so I don't reveal how I'm really feeling. But then I see his expression, and he looks *pleased*. He's happy that I'm angry. I release my grip on the chair and take a step back before I give in to the urge to pick it up and throw it at him.

"You look upset, kitten."

My nostrils flare. I decide to settle on the truth. "I am." I keep my hands straight so I don't ball them into fists. It won't do me any good to fight a man like him head on. I need to save my energy for when I'll *have* to fight him off, since I'm sure that's coming. I should also be adopting a more submissive tone considering I've come to terms with the fact that he's the only way I can get out of here. But I'm holding on to my anger. It's better than giving into the hopelessness of the situation.

"With me?" He tsks and shakes his head as he takes slow and deliberate steps toward me. I take another step back as he sets the plate down on the chair. "Don't be angry with me, kitten. I--"

"Stop calling me that!" I scream at him, hating how he's talking to me. Like he's placating a disobedient child.

His shoulders stiffen, and the soft angles of his face harden with anger. "Now now, you shouldn't speak to me that way. You're a smart girl, so you should know better." His tone is soothing, like he's trying to appease me, but it's right on the edge of taunting me with condescension.

"What do you want from me?" I ask with a choked voice. I want to get this part over with. That's really what I need to find out. I want to know what I have to do to get the fuck out of this room.

"I want you to submit to me," he answers simply.

"Fine." I whisper the word. I need to play along in order

to get the fuck out of here. I relax my shoulders, trying to channel a softer side of me.

He tilts his head and echoes, "Fine?" A low chuckle rises in his chest, and I have to keep my eyes wide open and my lips slammed shut to avoid showing how much it turns me on. What the fuck is wrong with me? My breathing picks up and I take another step back, not trusting him or my reactions.

"Alright, then...*kitten*." He stares at me, waiting for a response to his pet name for me. I don't give him one. Instead I hold my tongue and push down my pride. "Come over here and get down on your knees."

My heart sinks. I'm not doing that shit. He's out of his fucking mind if he thinks I'm going to suck him off. As much as I want to obey him so I can get the fuck out of here, I'm not going to do that. I'm not a whore. I could bite his dick off though. I feel my eyebrows raise at the thought, and the tiny cellar fills with a deep, rough laugh from the man standing across from me.

"You're adorable, kitten. But that's not going to happen. Not yet." He shakes his head with a small smile on his face.

"What's not going to happen?" I play dumb, like I wasn't that obvious just now.

"You haven't earned my touch yet, and you don't need it right now." He picks up the plate and moves the chair so it's facing me before sitting down. "Now come here and get on your knees so I can feed you."

I hesitate to move. I don't believe him, not for one second. And kneeling before him would put me at an even greater physical disadvantage.

"Come on, I know you're hungry." He sets the plate on his lap and motions with his fingers for me to come to him. "It's almost eleven, and you didn't eat last night. You must be starving."

My eyes narrow on him. I hate that he watched me last night. I knew it. I should have trusted my instincts. I knew someone was out there. "How long did you watch me?"

"I've been watching you ever since I got the hit on you." He's quick with his response, and it chills my blood.

"Are you a member of the mafia?" I ask.

He chuckles and says, "Which one?" The fact that he thinks this is funny really pisses me off.

"Are you a Cassano?" I ask with force.

"No. I'm not."

"So why are you going to kill me then?" My heart sinks. I don't understand. How many fucking people did I piss off?

"I'm not going to kill you," he says with a hard voice. His blue eyes turn dark and I can feel the weight of the conviction in his voice. "It took a lot for me to be able to have you. But I bought you from the Cassanos, and now I'm keeping you." I can't help that my pussy twitches at his words.

"Why?" my voice asks, without my conscious consent.

He leans forward slightly. "I've asked you twice now to come and get down on your knees. You need to learn to listen."

My feet move of their own accord until I'm standing in front of him. My legs tremble as I slowly kneel before him. I swallow thickly. Finally, I sit on my heels and keep my eyes on the door behind him. I have to do what needs to be done. My heart sinks and I just want to cry.

"Look at me, kitten," his deep voice commands me, and I look up at him reluctantly. I feel weak, and I hate it. Everyone assumes I'm weak. Now that I'm on my knees without a fight, it's hard for me to disagree. I look at his gorgeous face with nothing but sadness on mine.

"Don't be sad. You'll enjoy this." He leans forward and places a large hand on my shoulder. I fucking lean into his touch and close my eyes before I can stop myself. "Trust me."

My eyes harden at his words, but before I can spit back that I don't even know him, let alone trust him, he takes his hand away and says, "You'll learn to trust me."

I bite the inside of my cheek and wait for his next move. My eyes are drawn to his fingers as he reaches for a chunk of what I think is tuna. My mouth waters as he dips it into some sort of sauce and brushes it along the side of the cup until none of the sauce is dripping from the chunk of fish. He brings it to my lips and I instinctively lean back and move my hands up in front of my face.

The man's deep voice rings out. "No." My body jumps at his disapproval, and my heart races as I look into his eyes. Half of me still expects him to be violent toward me, even though he hasn't yet. "You know what I want."

He seems to relax some as he registers my fear. "Hands on your knees like they were, and mouth open. You were seated perfectly."

I obey him even though my fear seems to paralyze my body. I'm simply moving to his commands in order to survive. I have to admit him saying I was "seated perfectly" gives me a small thrill. And I fucking hate that. I wish he weren't having this reaction on me.

"Open," he commands, and I do as he says. He gently places the chunk of tuna in my mouth and as he does, my stomach grumbles from hunger.

He smiles down at me and dips another piece in the sauce. "I knew you were hungry, kitten." He looks at me again with curiosity, holding the piece over the plate. "Do you like it?"

My heart beats slowly as I search his face. I wonder if he's toying with me. If I admit that I like it, he might take it away and make me starve.

"I'd like you to answer me quickly and honestly, Catherine." His voice holds a note of admonishment, and I feel compelled to apologize.

"I'm sorry, s--" Sir is on the tip of my tongue, but I pause as I realize I don't know what to call him.

"Anthony," he says, answering my unspoken question. "No need to be sorry." His other hand grips my chin to get my attention. "You're learning. I can be reasonable so long as you're making an effort to obey. Is that understood?" he asks.

"Yes, Anthony."

"Good." His fingers stroke my jaw briefly. "Did you like that?" he asks.

"Yes...Anthony." It feels odd saying his name again so soon. But I imagine it's what he wants.

He smirks at me, the fucking bastard. "You don't have to say it every time." He holds the fish out and I open my mouth obediently.

It's so fucking good. It's not fair that I am fucking loving this fish. It's sweet, with a hint of spice. I'd eat this every day if I could. My eyes widen. He knew I'd like it. He smirks at me again as if reading my mind.

"Open," he says, holding out another piece.

I do as he says. And again and again. His fingers brush against my lips more and more. He puts a piece up to my mouth, and I take it and swallow before I realize his finger is still in front of my face.

"A bit of sauce, suck." My core heats and stirs as I maintain eye contact and open my mouth. His lips part as he slips his finger slowly into my mouth. I gently suck and massage him with my tongue. His eyes go half-lidded, and his breath comes in pants. And that's when I push my teeth down. Not hard, but enough that they scrape against him as he slowly pulls his finger free from my mouth. I know it didn't hurt him, but he got the message.

Once his finger is finally released, he grabs my jaw forcefully. He shoves his thumb into my mouth, tilting my head slightly. I'm forced to remain still, with my neck bent at an awkward angle. "Be a good girl, kitten. I know you could hurt me if you wanted to." He leans in closer and whispers in my ear. His hot breath sends shivers down my back. "Just remember, I could hurt you too, *if I wanted.*"

The threat makes me regret my action. My eyes fall, and tears prick the back of them as he releases me. My heart hurts, and anxiety races through me.

"Open." I hear him give his command, but I can't. I feel sick to my stomach. I fall back onto my heels and turn away from him. I can't. I can't do this. I back away slightly as he moves to the floor, setting the plate on the metal chair with a clink. Tears leak from my eyes.

"Hush, kitten," he says as he wraps his arms around me and pulls me against his chest. "I understand, I do." He rubs my back gently and it calms me. I lean into his touch, loving the warmth. It's been so fucking long since I've been held. Once I went into hiding, I was always alone in that house. It's made me weak.

"I don't want to hurt you. I want you to enjoy this, and I don't want you to be sad. But I don't want you to push me either. Not unless you *want* to be punished." I bury my head deeper into his chest, trying to resist how everything he's saying is making me want to play. This isn't pretend though.

There'll be no stopping this once it's started, and that terrifies me. But as much as I'd like to tell myself it hasn't started, I know it already has. And I'm playing into his hands.

The realization sobers me. I slowly back away and get back into a submissive position, although my eyes aren't on him at all. I stare at the floor and try to gather some kind of composure. I quickly wipe the tears away and chance a look at him as he sits back on the chair. He looks uncertain. It's an expression I haven't seen on him before. It makes me fucking terrified. He's quick to adjust the look on his face.

"Come," he says with a firm resolve. He pats his left leg. "Let's try this again." He waits patiently as I stand and sit awkwardly on his lap. His left arm wraps around my waist and he pulls me closer to him. Even though he's so tall compared to me, his head is nearly level with mine with us seated like this. He rests his left hand in my lap, dangerously close to my pussy. My nightgown has ridden up some and I feel exceptionally vulnerable. I'm stiff on his lap, and I can't relax with his hand where it is.

He waits a moment before saying or doing anything. It's awkward as fuck.

"You need to relax." He dips his finger into the sauce and brings it to my lips. He stares into my eyes rather than giving me the command. I do as he wants and open my mouth. He slips his finger past my lips. His eyes are drawn to my mouth as I gently suck his finger clean. When he pulls his finger away, he gives me a satisfied look.

"Good kitten." He puts another piece of the tuna tartare to my lips and I accept it. Seeing his approval eases something in me. I know so long as he's pleased, I'm safe with him. And so far, pleasing him is simple, but I don't know what other *terms* he has.

On the next bite, I find myself leaning into his fingers. He tsks and pulls the piece away from me. My heart rate speeds up until I realize what I've done to upset him. I swallow and sit back on my heels, exactly the way I was positioned before. His left hand runs along the thin fabric of my nightgown, just above my clit. "Good job, kitten." My pussy spasms around nothing. I close my eyes, hating how my body is betraying me. My nipples are hard, and the light brush of the fabric against them only turns me on even more. Other than his hand edging closer and closer to my pussy, he shows no signs of his own arousal.

"Eat until you're full." He grabs another piece, and we continue like this. Each time he feeds me his fingers brush a little closer to my throbbing clit, until finally his deft fingers are massaging small circles over my clit. I'm soaked for him, and primed for him to fuck me. And I fucking hate it. He's playing me and using my body against me.

He leans into my neck and whispers with his lips barely touching the shell of my ear, "I knew you'd like this. You just need to admit that you want it."

I'm not sure what angers me more--that I've allowed myself to be such easy prey for him, or that he's right. I want him to fuck me, and I fucking hate him for it. But I'm not going to let him reduce me to nothing but a whore.

I push away from him and kick the plate off his lap while I fall to the floor. The dish smashes on the ground as I fall backward.

He rises quickly, somewhat bracing my fall. The anger washing off of him is so strong that I scoot backward on my ass without even realizing at first. My heart races in my chest, and my blood rushes in my ears. Fear consumes me.

Making Anthony angry is something I shouldn't do. I know this as a truth, but I pissed him off anyway. I was going to play along. Why couldn't I just do what I needed to?

I expect him to hit me, or to grab me like he did earlier for my outburst. Inwardly I'm cursing myself for not just going along with this. But I can't. I'm more than *that*.

I anticipate his aggression. He doesn't get violent. Instead, he turns his back on me.

"I'm disappointed in you, kitten," he says as he carefully picks up several pieces of thick porcelain. He's slow to pick them up, and for a moment I imagine myself grabbing a single piece, the one closest to me. But I don't. I'm frozen with fear. After a moment of him cleaning up the mess I made, he looks me in the eyes as he picks up the last shard.

He turns to the door with an expression of discontent and that's when I realize he's leaving me.

My racing heart tries to leap from my chest. I can't be left here. I need to get out. "Please don't leave me here!" I scream and beg. I didn't want to, but I have to try. I don't want him to leave me here alone. I can't sit here with nothing. No plan, no hope, fucking nothing.

"I'm sorry, kitten," he says as he turns his back on me. "Tonight training will begin. It's best that you put this rebellion behind you. You won't enjoy being punished."

Tonight? How fucking long will I have to wait in this room alone?

"I have a life! Please just let me go!" I feel weak and hate what I've become.

"I know you do, kitten. And I would provide for you in every way you need."

"I want *my* life back!" I don't want to be his version of a pampered pet. I want my job and my friends. I worked hard to create this new life for myself, and I want it back. I don't want it torn from me.

He turns back to me with anger sparking in his eyes. It's enough to make me retreat until my back hits the wall. He strides toward me with a dark aura surrounding him.

"You want an office? You want to go online so you can work? Do you want your books, kitten?" I stare at him, not knowing what to say.

"I told you to answer me when I ask you a question," he says with barely contained anger.

"Yes. Yes, that's what I want." I answer him in a strangled voice I don't recognize.

He smirks at me, and that expression is completely at odds with the aggression choking the air between us. "You would've had all of that, if only you'd behaved." I stare at him with disbelief as he makes his way back to the door.

He's lying. He must be. I can't help but hope.

"Please. Just another chance." I take a hesitant step forward as he punches the code into the keypad.

He turns to face me with sympathy in his eyes. "We'll try again at dinner." Before he leaves me alone again, he turns to face me. "I'm going easy on you right now, but remember this is only because it's your first day and we haven't discussed terms yet." He looks at me expectantly as I wipe the angry tears from my eyes.

"I expect you to answer me," he says with the hint of a threat in his voice. "You will look at me when I'm speaking to you."

My eyes dart around as my breath catches in my throat. I don't even remember what he said. My mouth parts, but words don't come out.

He takes long, quick strides toward me, letting the door fall shut behind him. I cower and find my back up against the wall again. He stops inches away from me like last time, but this time he grips the nape of my neck and pulls me toward him.

"I want you so fucking badly." His low voice sends a chill down my body. "I want to show you how good this is going to be." His fingers tangle in my hair, and he makes a fist at the base of my head, forcing me to expose my neck to him.

He leans forward, pressing his body against mine and his large erection digs into my belly. Being held like this sends a need coursing through my body. Every nerve ending is on alert and ready to spark to life. I clench my thighs as my nipples harden.

He leaves an open-mouthed kiss on my neck. It's so gentle, and so at odds with everything else.

"You'll learn to obey me, kitten, and you'll fucking love it when you do." His hand pushes between my legs and he cups my pussy. His lips brush against my ear as he whispers. "I will give you everything you need. Everything you want. But you need to submit to me." His hot breath gently caressing my sensitive skin forces a moan from my lips. He takes my earlobe into his mouth and gently nips it. "You're going to beg me to fuck you, kitten. I'll wait for it. I'll wait for you to beg me."

With that, he leaves me. My body sags against the wall and the chill of the damp cell replaces his warmth. I take in a ragged breath and barely catch sight of him as he leaves me cold and alone. I watch the door close quickly behind him, like he couldn't get out fast enough.

I close my eyes, hating that I'm so turned on by him. I shouldn't be. All of this is wrong in every way. Even worse, I hate that I already crave his touch.

CHAPTER 6

ANTHONY

I hear the door shut with a loud click and lean back, reveling in how perfect she is. She's caught up in her own mind and holding back, but she's exactly how I dreamed she'd be.

It's going to be so fucking good when she finally lets go. I need to break those walls down and I'm doing that as soon as fucking possible. Fuck patience. She needs a push. She's desperate to get out of that room and I can't blame her. Come tonight, if I don't let her out, she'll be sleeping on a hard as fuck floor. I don't want that for her, and I don't want her in that cell. But I don't have a choice. She needs to learn.

The thought brings to mind the memory of her scraping her teeth against my finger. If I'm honest with myself, it was hot as hell. I love how brazen she is, but she knew what she was doing.

She had to be punished. There's a lot of research on the psychology of motivation via punishment and reward. Reward is always better, but when punishment needs to happen it's best if the severity of the punishment is in direct proportion to the offense. Ideally it should also be swift, taking place as soon as possible after the misdeed. If you merely give a slap on the wrist, the behavior is more than likely to occur again, and also more likely to be a worse transgression.

I needed that punishment to be aggressive to keep her from pushing. But I didn't like that I had to do it. It's better now that it's over with. Hopefully things will continue to go as planned, and the next time she pushes it'll be minimal. And that way I can get my hands on her ass and move this along to other forms of play.

My fingers twitch with the need to touch her again. I don't know if she noticed how she rocked her cunt against my hand. I know she was hot and wet from what we did, and she should have been. There's nothing wrong with being turned on by what happened. It's natural.

I just need to break down the social constructs she has built in her head. She has to learn to give in to her needs and desires. She has to learn to trust that I'm gonna give her everything she could ever want. The life she's built; she can have it. But I can add so much more. I can let her give in to her own dark desires and show her a world she's only dreamed of. I'll teach her that. Tonight I'll give her a test, and if she obeys the one command I give her, I'll let her out of that room. That will be huge for us. I only hope she doesn't disappoint me.

She's too headstrong and preoccupied with right and wrong. She knows she wants this, but I don't think a girl like her gives into desires. She's strict in her regimen, and doesn't reward herself much. I'll have to ease her into enjoying this, one reward at a time.

I make my way to the dining room where I left my phone and cringe when I see I've missed messages. Three are from Vince. I put my password in and take a look. The first and most recent text is from Tommy, my brother, but also my partner in the hits.

Cassys have another for us.

Cassys are the Cassanos. Ever since we started taking on outside hits, they've been good customers. Apparently they get pissed off. A lot.

The next three are from Vince. It looks like he sent them within minutes of each other, and the first one arrived almost immediately after my last message to him.

They seem to be under a different impression.

They want a timeline.

We're talking tonight.

Fuck. I don't like any of the shit in those messages. I don't really give a fuck what impression the Cassanos are under. I bought her freedom from them. If they changed their minds, that's on them. I don't have to do shit for them, and neither does Vince.

I finally text back, *I paid for this shipment.*

What the fuck am I supposed to tell them? he asks, and I can practically hear his anger.

The deal's done. I tell him simply.

I know we do a lot of business with them, but I don't like where Vince's head is at. He's the Don and even though technically Tommy and I aren't included in the *familia* shit, we're not fooling anyone. He's the boss, and we're still untouchables. We're still family and *familia* and nothing changes that. It also means I have to listen to the fuck. Usually I agree with him. But on this? No. I don't fucking like the way he's talking.

What do you need from me? I ask after a moment.

I need a timeline.

I stare at the phone. I don't know what to say. I never had one in mind. And I sure as fuck don't plan on making one now.

I don't have one. Your call.

I send the text, knowing full well that whatever deadline he gives me, I'm going to try to and extend it. The phone goes off, but I don't look at it. I'll figure this shit out later. Nothing is going to ruin this for me.

I put the phone down and leave it there, knowing damn

well I'm not going to like anything he has to say about this. I need to get started on something to eat tonight and make sure her room is set up.

I don't want to get my hopes up, but I have a good feeling that she's going to pass this test. I fucking hope she does. She desperately needs to cum. My eyes fly to the door to the basement. Fuck! I didn't tell her she wasn't allowed to touch herself without my permission. Fuck me, I didn't tell her anything.

She's a smart girl though, and she's read a lot of dirty books. She should know better.

She had better know better.

CHAPTER 7

CATHERINE

I'm fucking rocking like a crazy person. I could sit in the chair, but it's tainted now. So instead I'm huddled in the corner rocking. It's not because I'm crazy though. It's because there isn't a fucking thing to do, not a damn thing to do in this empty cell.

I've walked around every inch of this room. Even though it's dark, the cell's not too dirty. I should know, since I've searched everywhere for a second door, or crack, or opening. Anything. I bet he watched me; in the books, they always watch. I even expect some kind of punishment for it, but I had to do it. I had to try.

All the flashbacks keep coming forward, and I keep

pushing them down. They make me weak. I can't go back to that. He's not one of them.

"Come on, little mouse," Lorenzo says as he parks his car in front of the restaurant.

"I don't want to." I already told him I don't want to, but he's not listening.

He has his dick out and he's pushing me to go down on him here, but there are people everywhere. At first when we met, I was looking for that thrill. But we kept getting caught by his friends, and now they give me weird looks and make jokes that I don't like.

He moves faster than me, and it takes me by surprise. He fists my hair and yanks my head back. I scream out in pain and try to pry his hand off of me. "Stop, it hurts." Tears prick my eyes. "It hurts!" I scream out.

"Dumb bitch," he says under his breath. "You know what you got yourself into. You fucking want it this way." My heart sinks in my chest. I don't want it, and especially not like this.

"Suck it," he says, releasing me while pushing my head forward. I look back at him with daggers in my eyes.

"Fuck you," I sneer at him, and wipe my eyes. He barks out a laugh.

"Aw, little mouse. You don't want to play?" I feel sick to my stomach. Things never used to be like this. When he's rough with me in bed now, it's different, too.

"I said no." I hate that I have to tell him twice.

"Fine," he says as he tucks himself back into his pants and I feel a small sense of relief.

"Come here, you know I didn't mean it." He leans across the console to give me a kiss and I hesitate, but I lean in anyway. Because I'm a fucking idiot. Because I thought I just needed to make the lines clearer. Like it was my fault.

That was right before I tried to leave him. I had no one else, and I was afraid to be alone. I was so desperate for his "love" that I stayed with that fucking creep far too long. Things only got worse after that. I remember the night I tried to sneak out and run away. Before I left, I looked down on his sleeping body and thought about slitting his throat. How awful of a person had I become where I thought I should kill him? Not fucking awful at all. That bastard deserved to die. But I couldn't do it. I couldn't lower myself to becoming a murderer, so instead I sneaked out through a window and hoped I could start over. Instead I fell right into a new world of hell.

I hear them laugh as Lorenzo backhands me again. This time I fall. I learned to make it look real.

When he was drunk that's the game he played. How many hits until the mouse would fall? He liked his nickname for me even more after I saw what happened. He was daring me, taunting me to be a *rat*. If I stayed on the ground, he'd only kick me a few times. I learned to just stay curled on my side and wait for the beatings to be over, no matter how much he urged me to stand. He only made it worse if I obeyed him. Bruises gave way to broken bones, but by then, I had no way to leave. I was trapped and beaten regularly for his enjoyment. I barely escaped them. And I only managed because they were reckless. Their desires to cause me even more pain is what eventually gave me my out.

They came into the room they kept me in. It'd only been a few days of being trapped there, feeling helpless and weak, trying to recover from the beating he gave me. The three of them came into the room and left the door wide open as they stalked to my bed. I knew what they were going to do. I rock harder, remembering the fear. I fucking bolted. I just kept thinking, *Please don't let them catch me.*

They can never catch me. Never. I had to do everything I could to escape that hell. But I had no one. Not a single soul to run to. My mother was everyone and everything to me. But she'd been dead for nearly a year. I ran to her grave and prayed for a sign. That's when the cops showed up, sirens blaring. I thanked my mom every day.

I thought she'd saved me like she always did.

But they did catch me.

Only they didn't come after me directly like I thought they would. They sent someone else.

I have no clue how long it's been. I don't know what he's doing. Or what this training is going to be like when he gets back. I have absolutely no control in any of it either, and I don't like it. I tug at the hem of my nightgown, wishing it were longer so I could cover myself up more. My knees are drawn up to my chest, and I rest my head on them as I consider my next step.

I don't know what to do. I don't know what my options are. He said he'd give me my life and everything I needed. I want to believe that's true, but what's the catch? I know his intentions aren't pure. And I'm certain his terms aren't negotiable.

I'm eager to hear what he has to say though. I want to know what I've gotten myself into. That way I can figure out how to get the fuck out of here.

My back is killing me, so I keep up my rocking. It feels better than just sitting still for however fucking long it's been. I'd get up and stretch or do yoga, but I don't want to be standing when he walks in. I want to be ready.

Well, as ready as I can be.

I close my eyes and remember his words. An office, my books. How much does he know about me? He's been watching me, obviously. I wonder if there were signs I missed. Red flags I should have seen, but didn't.

The only time I ever felt that things were off was last night. That was the only chance I had. I should have gotten into my car and driven away. I should have listened to my gut.

But I didn't.

I've never felt so fucking helpless. Not when I was with

Lorenzo. Not when I was taken by those fucking Cassanos. Not even when I went to the police and they told me I'd have to leave my old life behind forever. Never. Because there was always hope. But now, I only have his word. And I don't trust him.

For all I know, he has a bet going with someone. How long would it take him to get into my pants willingly? And then boom. He'll kill me. Or he'll let someone else in here to have a go at me. How the fuck would I know? I don't know shit. And it's not like he's offering up any information. He's just playing this game with me.

In all the books I've read, there's been some sort of contract, or list. Terms. Like he said before.

That always happens first.

But he's playing with me. Testing me. And as far as I'm concerned, he's winning.

My body betrayed me, and I gave into the weakness. I was practically ready to cum on his lap. If he'd flipped me over and put his mouth on my clit rather than whispering in my ear, shit. I don't know what I would have done. I was so weak. So desperate.

It's pathetic. *I'm* pathetic.

But what real choice do I have? I can fight his game, or I can play along. I can stay here and let him toy with me, or I can use him to get out of here.

Use him.

I like that idea. It almost makes the desire for him to

touch me feel justified. That giving in and caving to his touch is alright. I'm merely playing into his hand because it's what I have to do.

As if hearing my thoughts, Anthony opens the door.

My breath stills in my lungs as the loud click echoes off the walls.

I make a promise to myself. I'll do whatever I have to do to get the fuck out of this room. I need to see if I can trust his word at least.

Just as I make that promise to myself, I see what he's pulling behind him. It's a large bench with leather shackles. Fuck! Tears prick my eyes.

I bury my head in my knees and just fucking cry. He's going to chain me to the bench. He's going to fuck me.

A wretched sob heaves through my chest.

I shake my head, and that's when I hear his footsteps. But I don't back away. I have no options. What choice do I have?

CHAPTER 8

ANTHONY

I turn around as soon as I hear her crying.

Fuck. I wanted to shock her, but I didn't think she'd cry.

She had so much fight in her when I left her. I don't know what happened while I was gone. I know that being alone for hours can be torturous when you have nothing. No noise but the sounds you make, nothing to touch but yourself and the walls and floor.

But I didn't think it would affect her like this.

"Kitten," I begin as I crouch down next to her, although I keep my distance. She could be playing me for a fool. Waiting for me to comfort her so she can strike. I'm certain I picked up the large chunks of the plate. There were only three or four of them. But maybe she found a smaller piece and she's planning to stab the shit out of me with it. She doesn't trust me, and I sure as fuck don't trust her.

I didn't watch her in the monitor. I was driving myself crazy watching her do nothing. More than anything seeing her like that pissed me off, because all I wanted to do was to go to her. But she's being punished.

This is a part of her punishment.

"Yes, Anthony," she answers in a strangled voice. She raises her head with tears staining her reddened cheeks. I'm surprised she answered. She wipes the tears from her face and I see she doesn't have anything in her hands. She's not armed, and she's not trying to fight me. She's just genuinely upset.

"Why are you crying?" I ask her.

"Because I give up. I'll let you do whatever you want. I just want this to end." My heart stops in my chest. That's not at all what I expected, and so far she's done everything I thought she would.

I haven't broken her yet. But maybe I've taken away her hope of getting out of here unless she obeys.

"And that makes you sad?" I ask to clarify. "You're upset that you're giving me control?" Truthfully though, she never had any control. Maybe over her own actions, but not at all over the situation. She's a strong woman. I guess that very realization could be troubling her.

She takes in a small gasp and shakes her head. "Of course

I'm upset about that. Normal people don't do this."

Although I appreciate her honesty, that fucking attitude is going to be the first thing I correct.

"Watch your mouth, kitten." She looks up at me with nothing in her eyes.

"Yes, Anthony. I'm sorry, sir." She says the words without a hint of sarcasm in her voice. And it's disappointing. I'm surprised by my reaction to it.

"Could I know the terms, please? Before you chain me?" she asks in a flat voice. It's unsettling how much I don't like it.

"No." I watch her as I answer sternly. She merely nods her head slowly, as if she figured I wouldn't tell her anything.

"Okay." Her voice is small and she's finished crying. She sniffles once and nods her head again. "I'm ready."

I was foolish to think that this behavior didn't indicate her inner strength. She's resigning herself to a fate she doesn't want so that she can move forward. That in and of itself is strong. I feel my tense muscles relax now that I understand.

I grip her chin with my thumb and forefinger and make her look me in the eyes.

"You won't regret this, Catherine. I promise you." As I say the words with confidence, I remember Vince and the Cassanos, and I fucking hate myself for thinking of them right now. I won't let them take her. And I won't let her regret this either.

"I'm going to put you on the bench, and I want you to hold onto the straps." She nods her head and then whispers,

"Yes, Anthony."

"Once you agree to the terms, and only then, I'll bind your wrists."

She closes her eyes and I can see her pride leave completely as shame overwhelms her. I knew this would happen. But I still don't like it. This isn't the part of this relationship that I looked forward to. But the next part, the part where she learns she can trust me and that it's not the nightmare she perceives it to be? That part will be worth all of this.

"Up, kitten." I stand up and hold a hand out for her. She starts to get up on her own, but then she sees my hand. She looks dejected and depressed. That's exactly what she is. Depressed that she's given in to me. But I'm going change that. I'm going to make her love giving in to me.

I walk her over to the bench and help her on. I fucking love this idea. It's meant for spanking and fucking, and I intend to do both in time. But for now, that's not what we're going do. I lay her down so that her chest is flat against the lowered part and her ass is in the air. Her eyes are focused on the leather binds.

I take one strap out and hold it for her to take. "Go on, kitten. It won't magically wrap around your wrist." Again her eyes meet mine and I see a spark of the smart-mouthed woman from this morning. But it's only a dim flicker of defiance, and she takes the leather without much hesitation. She does the same with the right without my help. She lays her head and body flat with her legs and hand off the side. She waits for my next command with her pussy almost fully bared to me, covered only by a thin layer of fabric.

She's perfect like this, vulnerable and waiting for me. But she's obviously unhappy and only doing it because the other choice isn't really a choice at all. I splay my hand on her back, and although she stiffens, she doesn't move away from my touch. I walk around her slowly, moving my hand in soothing circles until she slowly relaxes her body.

I keep my voice soft and comforting. "The terms are simple. You do your best to obey me. If you don't, you come back here." Her eyes close as I speak. "If you please me, I will reward you. I will give you everything you need. You want your old life, and you can have it." Her eyes fly to mine, but before she can question me I add, "I will simply be a new constant in that life." Her eyes fall to the floor and then close again.

She whispers, "Yes, Anthony. I understand." That was too easy.

"You don't have any questions?" I'm surprised by that.

"What questions should I ask?" My dick finally starts hardening. Her submission is just now starting to arouse me.

"Any questions you have, kitten. I'll answer them all truthfully."

"If I do this, you'll let me out of this room? You said I'd have an office and my old life back?"

"Yes, that's right."

"I'll be able to keep working?" she asks.

"You will," I reply. I walk around to where her head is and place my hand on her chin to make sure she sees my face and knows how serious I am. "It will be heavily monitored though. And any sign that you've disobeyed me by doing anything at all that would obviously upset me will result in you being sent here. And not just for a few hours, kitten."

She nods her head and says, "I understand."

"Anything else?" I ask.

She shakes her head. "No."

"You don't want to know what I'm going to do with you?" I ask. I imagine she's already made up her mind.

"You're going to do what you'd like to me." Her voice is flat, but dampened by sadness.

"Close," I answer. "I'd love to fuck you, kitten. But I've told you I won't do that until you beg." Her head lifts slightly off the bench and her eyes widen with hope. That's the woman I want with me. Her reaction makes me smile.

"You thought I was going to fuck you right now?" I ask her.

"Yes," she answers with a tinge of confusion.

"I told you I wasn't going to until you begged. I mean it," I say.

"Do I have to let you do that in order to get out of here?" she asks.

"No," I answer, and love how much her body relaxes at my answer. I love it because she's showing trust in my words.

I'm giving her hope and her strength back. Even if she doesn't realize that.

"Will I ever have to...?" she starts to ask, but trails off. My eyebrows raise and I lay a hand on the small of her back.

"I want to reward you as a dom should reward his submissive." I let my hands travel to her ass. I cup her cheeks and spread them slightly. "I'll let you know if I'd like to be pleasured. But it'll be your choice if you'd like to give me that." I let my thumbs skim along the seam in the center of her panties.

"I do want to reward you, kitten. Do you know what that means?" I ask.

She nods her head, seeming very much at ease with the knowledge I've given her.

"Tell me what you think it means."

It takes her a moment to respond, but when she does, I'm pleased. "It's what you were doing earlier."

I smile at her backside as my fingers slip past her panties. I run them along her slick heat and I'm rewarded with a soft moan.

"You rubbed my clit," she says as she continues her answer.

"Why?" I ask as I gently place her panties back where they belong.

"To reward me," she says.

"What was I rewarding?" I ask her. I'm sure she'll say it's because she was listening to me. Or because she did as she was told. But in actuality it's because she was enjoying it. I rewarded her desire for my control to continue. I'm intentionally conditioning her reactions and her emotions.

"Because I listened to you and obeyed. Because I earned it." She adds the last part forcefully. I smirk behind her. That's how that dirty book went about it. You obey, and you get rewarded. Disobey, and you get punished.

I agree to an extent, but emotions are far more powerful a tool. She'll thrive with my touch. She'll love my control. And it'll only bring her happiness.

"I want to reward you now, kitten. Should I?" I ask her.

Yes. Yes, I fucking should. But right now I want her permission. I want her to control this next step. If she answers yes, I'll have her shackled and cumming harder than she ever has before. If she'd prefer not, that's fine, but I won't shackle her. I'll merely move to her room, unrewarded in some ways, but feeling safe in others. It's a fair trade. And either way, she's rid of this room so long as she isn't disobedient.

After a quiet moment, I look at her face. She seems lost in contemplation.

"I think so," she finally answers. I chuckle at her response.

"You're being very good, kitten. How would you like me to reward you?"

She bites down on her bottom lip.

"I--" she starts to speak, but stops herself. I know she's ready. I know she's craving a release. Each time I rest a hand gently on her lush ass, she tilts it slightly.

"Tell me, kitten. I want you to know that you can tell me anything. So long as you're respectful, you won't be punished."

"I don't want you to...have sex with me." Hearing those words fall from her lips is disappointing. But I simply tack on the unspoken "yet" to the end. Obviously she won't admit that she wants me just yet. She's angling for control as well. This is her bid to ensure that if she says no, it's not going to happen. And that's a truth. I want to earn it. I want her to yearn for my touch and desire pleasing me more than anything else. And I will. This is just a step, a small hurdle, in that direction.

"I don't intend on fucking you. Not until you *beg* me, remember?" She eyes me warily and I know I should just play my cards so she has more confidence in her decision. I reach inside my pocket and pull out a small vibrator.

"You're doing very well, kitten. I'll be honest, I'm very pleased. But you haven't earned my touch yet." Her brows creases and she almost looks disappointed. "This is all I'll use." She looks between my face and the vibrator.

"You're going to tease me? Until I beg." It pisses me off that she makes that assumption. Although I know she's read that shit in her books.

"No. That would not be a reward. I'm going to put this vibrator against your clit and make you rock yourself on it until you cum. That's all there is to your reward."

She may not notice that her ass raises just slightly, but I

sure as fuck do.

"I asked you a question. Do you think you should be rewarded?"

"Yes." She finally gives me the green light in a breathy voice that makes my dick impossibly hard.

"I think so too, kitten." I push the vibrator under her, past her clit and snug between her body and the bench, just to warm it and then walk around to the front of the bench. I take the strap in her left hand and move it into place. She pulls back and nearly falls off the bench. "This is your reward, but you will receive it how I see fit."

Her big brown eyes look up at me with worry. I can't wait to ease her concerns.

"I told you what's going to happen. I won't lie. Once you've cum, I'm going to want you, and I'll ask. But if you say no, or don't beg well enough, I'll release you and show you to your room." She nods her head and places her chest flat on the bench again. Her breathing is coming in pants and I know she's scared. But she's trusting me. In only a day, I've gained enough trust to make her bared to me, completely vulnerable--and she did so willingly.

The realization thrills me.

I strap both her wrists and her ankles, letting my fingers trail along her exposed skin. I gently pull the nightgown up to her waist and then slip her panties slowly down her thighs. They don't go far, but it's enough to expose her. I bend slightly and blow against her glistening sex. She's so fucking wet. I want to lean in and take a languid lick of her sweet cunt. I want to slide my fingers inside and feel her tight walls clench as she cums. But right now, I'm limited. Soon. Soon, she'll beg me for more. She'll desire nothing else. I smile as I pull away and pull out the warmed vibrator and twist it on.

Soon, she'll be begging me.

CHAPTER 9

CATHERINE

I pull my wrist slightly, but I can hardly move. My arms don't even bend. The leather straps around my wrist have virtually no give. My ankles are strapped as well and I can barely move my legs at all. I'm completely restrained. My heart beats frantically as his hands move down my body. My ass is higher up and I know why. This bench was made for fucking. And I'm strapped to it. Willingly.

As soon as he locked in the first buckle, I felt regret. I don't know him. He's not a good man. That's really all I'm sure of, at least about him. I know one other thing. I have to do this in order to get out of here. And he promised he would let me out. He's made all sorts of pretty promises. My blood heats as his hand lingers on my ass. His other hand moves to the other cheek and he spreads them. I can't help that I'm turned on. I'm so fucking hot for him. It's been over a year now since I've felt a man's hands on me. And I've definitely never felt the hands of a man like Anthony. It's exhilarating.

I'm wet and hot and desperate for his touch. It's sick. I shouldn't want this, but I do.

And he knows it. My cheeks flame with embarrassment. My pussy is fully exposed to him and I'm completely vulnerable. The only sounds I can hear are my own ragged breath and the humming of the vibrator. My lips part and I hold back a moan as he gently pushes it against my pussy lips, just beneath my clit.

"Are you an over or under girl, kitten?" he asks in a sexy-as-fuck voice while putting slightly more pressure against me. I instinctively try to pull away. The intensity is just too much. He moves the vibrator over my clit, and my entire body heats and tingles. The pit of my stomach stirs with a hot, radiating pleasure. My ass bucks up, but the rest of my body remains in place due to the restraints.

"Ah, over it is."

I whimper and turn my head from side to side. I've never felt something like this. It's too intense. My body's pleading to move away as the sensation grows and grows and my legs quiver. "Stay still. You're going to enjoy this," he whispers.

I try to keep my body from wanting to move, but it's useless.

"Move your hips, kitten." I instantly obey him, wanting and needing to move. The motion sends a surge of arousal to my core and soft gasps fall from my lips. I grind harder, loving the intensity of the pulses shooting through me. Close, so close. My neck arches back as I desperately search for my release.

His large hand splays on my lower back and pushes me down harder onto the vibrator. His force is what does it; I cum violently and scream out as the waves of pleasure roll through my body. The first wave is the most intense, then the rest grow dimmer and dimmer. My body feels limp on the table as I take in deep, uneven breaths.

"Have you ever used a vibrator before, kitten?" I shake my head no, and try to answer aloud, but he starts talking before I can respond. "You obviously enjoy the stimulation."

I nod my head and breathe out as I agree. "Yes." I swallow thickly, realizing I'm still pinned down. My eyes open a little more and I look at him to my left as he looks from my bared pussy to my face.

"Do you want to cum again?" he asks.

My breath stalls in my chest. I do want that again. But not from him, not now. I only did that so I can get the fuck out of here.

"You do, but not like this," he says. I break eye contact, hating how obvious I am. But then again, anyone else in my position would be this fucking obvious.

"Time to see your new room." he says, shutting off the

vibrator. He reaches down and unstraps the bands. I stay still, feeling uneasy yet relaxed at the same time. I want to be tense and on guard. But I'm too exhausted from all the shit I've been through. He unstraps the last restraint and I try to brace myself on the bench, but his hand comes down on my shoulders, pushing me back down.

It sets off every red flag. My heart beats faster and fear sets in.

"Let me pick you up. Your legs are still trembling." His voice is calming and soothing. I instantly feel myself relax. At the realization, I throw my guard up even higher.

I blink a few times to clear my head. I feel drunk on lust and pleasure. I breathe in deep as his arms tilt my body and he cradles me against his chest. He gently sets my feet down, but holds onto my waist. I want to push him away. I don't need his help. My legs are shaky, but I'm fine. It was just one orgasm, for crying out loud. One intense, earth-shattering orgasm, but still. I can manage on my own.

I'm sure as fuck not going to tell him that though. I just need to be good so I can get out of here and see where he's taking me. His body brushes against mine as he releases me. My eyes nearly close as I feel his massive erection through his jeans. I have to bite the inside of my cheek as my thighs clench and my pussy clamps down around nothing. I trap the moan in my throat.

His hand grips my shoulder and he leans down, placing a

kiss on my shoulder before whispering, "You alright?" I can practically feel his smile.

He knows exactly what he's doing. Instead of telling him off, I continue to play the role. That's what I need to do now. "Yes, Anthony."

He lets out a deep chuckle as he reaches into his pocket and pulls out a piece of black silk cloth. He holds it up with both hands and that's when I realize it's a blindfold.

Fuck. I was hoping I'd be able to see where we're going so I can get the layout of this place. I need to come up with a plan to get out of here. I'm sure the next room will be locked as well though, and then what? I'll be fucking stuck there, just like I am now. *He promised though.* I hate that I'm relying on his word. But I am. His word is the only hope I have.

My lips press into a hard line and his response is to smirk at me and raise a brow.

"Come on kitten, behave." His tone is playful and it makes me hate him even more. It's like we're playing cat and mouse, but he's always two steps ahead of me. I swallow my pride and turn around so he can place the cloth over my eyes.

I have no other option but to trust him. And I fucking hate it.

CHAPTER 10

ANTHONY

My little kitten thinks she's slick. It's fucking adorable. I can practically hear her thoughts. I know all of this is an act, but for a moment, I had her. I had a sweet submissive who trusted me and craved my touch. I want more.

I tighten the sash over her eyes and take a step back. Her arms move out slightly, as though she's off-balance. Without me there to guide her, I'm sure she is. Her mouth parts, but then she closes it and moves her hands to her side.

Good girl. She's trying hard to obey. I know it's only so she can use me. She's not doing it because she *wants* to. Not yet, anyway. But we'll get there. I just need to be patient.

I put my hands on her shoulders so she knows I'm there,

and then let them fall to her hips.

"Walk with me and hold my hand." I take her small hand in mine and slowly lead her to the door. Her other hand opens and closes. I know she'd like to reach for the blindfold. But she doesn't. Not yet. It won't do her any good to get it off though. Even if she does manage to get it off and race up the stairs somehow without me on right on her ass, she'd just come to another lock. And the combinations to enter her rooms are all different.

The entire basement is soundproofed. She could scream all she wanted, but she would be locked down here. The doors are programmed to unlock after three days though, if anything were to prevent me from returning to the house.

I punch in the code and lead her through the door. Her right hand twitches, and I know she's fighting the urge to bolt. She's working hard to stay by my side and not take off.

But ultimately she obeys. It's a fucking relief. Also, quite an achievement. A dozen or more scenarios played out in my mind, ranging from her starving herself to her throwing the chair at me. But this is nearly all I could hope for. It's perfect really. She's still resistant, but cooperating. I knew she'd be like this. She's perfect.

She's making it easy while still being a challenge. I like that. No, I fucking love that.

We get to her bedroom and I punch in the code. I see her shoulders sag slightly and the corners of her mouth turn down. She should be smarter than to think I'd place her in a room without a lock. I'm sure she knows better than that.

As soon as the door shuts behind us, I take off the sash. She blinks a few times before letting the astonishment show on her face. I look over her body and realize how unkempt she looks. Her skin's still flushed and gorgeous, save for a few smudges on her face. But her feet are bare and dirty, and her hair's tangled and in need of a wash. Even her nightgown looks rumpled and dirty on the part covering her ass since she sat on the floor most of the day. She was only in the cell for one day, but one was enough for her to get this disheveled. I'm not looking forward to having to send her back there, but I know she's going back. It's only a matter of time.

I made sure her room was spacious and would satisfy her every need and desire. It's a combination of her bedroom and living room. The en-suite is to the left, through a pair of large antique doors, and to the right she has an office that's accessible through another locked door. I hope that will be hers one day. For now, all contact she makes with the outside world will be monitored. I made sure to take her phone with me when I left. She hasn't received any messages or calls yet, but her social media shit is fucking constant. I have my ways to ensure we'll both be happy as far as that's concerned.

This room that I've prepared for her is nearly the size of her entire cabin. It takes up the majority of my basement. But she needs the space since this is all she'll have from now on.

I tried to section it off for her so she'd have a clear separation between the living room and bedroom. It's all the same soft grey in color though, which helps to unite the spaces. Most of the linens are white, giving it a very clean and modern look. The accents are pink though. Very pale pink. I even hung floor-to-ceiling crushed velvet curtains for her. They're only covering small windows that hardly let in any light, but they make the room look larger and more luxurious. I'm hopeful that everything is to her taste. Every piece I selected reminded me of her. I want this to be a dream come true, and the setting is every bit as important as the story.

In reality, her new home is much nicer than her cabin. Everything is new and fresh. I wanted everything to have the same feel as her cabin, just with more luxurious furnishings and decor. A huge bookshelf is in one corner. Some of the books are favorites of hers, but the others are my choices. I even brought her laptop for her so that she can keep working. Of course she'll only have access to it when I'll be present for now, and I installed a tracker and a logger so I'll be able to remotely monitor her, but she should still be thrilled to have it.

I watch her as she walks to each item, putting her hand out, but barely touching the furniture. She seems shocked, but also pleased, and that makes me happy. I'm proud that I can provide for her. I want that. I want her to see how good I can be for her.

She walks slowly to the table in front of the sofa. It's where

I set her Kindle. The tablet's in its case, and she pauses as she recognizes it as hers. Her eyes widen, and she looks back at me.

"I told you I'd give you what you need. And I understand your needs," I say. I know all of her needs, and I can't fucking wait to fuck her exactly how she needs it. She looks at me hesitantly, but I don't give her a moment to respond.

"You will obey me." Now's the time for me to start going over the terms since she's seen the alternative. "You will do what I say, when I say. I'll do my best to be reasonable and keep your limits in mind." I smirk and add a touch of humor to lighten the severity of the situation. Her eyes remain clouded with worry. I can tell she's thinking there's a catch beyond what I've told her. "But I will push you, and you will obey. If you don't at least try to obey me, you'll be punished, and this room will be taken from you."

I give her a moment to digest what I've told her.

"You said..." She pauses to clear her throat before continuing. "You said I would have to agree?" I nod.

"On physically pleasing me, yes. I only want your touch if you're eager to give it to me." That's absolutely true. I have no interest in taking my pleasure from her, I want her to give it to me freely.

She nods her head in understanding, appearing a bit more relaxed, but still unsure.

"Kitten, I have desires. And I want you to fulfill them." My hand burns with the need to touch her soft skin. "When I come into the room, I want you to kneel and wait for my command. My needs will be your priority." I want her submission more than anything. I want her to need me, and to look forward to my company. I need her complete trust. I will earn it.

Her breath comes in short pants, and I'm hoping this is turning her on more than anything else.

"Yes, Anthony," she answers in a respectful low tone.

"You can speak freely, so long as you're respectful. But I will punish that smart mouth of yours if you back talk or raise your voice to me. Is that understood?" I keep my voice soft, but firm as I face her. I want to brush her hair off her shoulder and wipe the smudges off her face. She needs to be cleaned and pampered.

She nods her head and says, "Yes. I understand." Her body language tells me everything I need to know. She's scared, and she doesn't trust a word I'm saying. She'll learn though. She just needs time. She needs space as well. I can't rush this fantasy. Deep down, she wants this. I'll still be here when she's ready for it. Until then, I'll have to control my own needs and desires.

"Now," I begin, as I walk to the soft grey sofa and pat the seat next to me as I sit down. She listens and quickly sits with her hands in her lap. Her eyes keep dancing around the room, so I wait for her full attention. It doesn't take long, which pleases me.

"I want to go over your earlier behavior," I say.

Her eyes widen slightly and she inhales deeply. I keep my

face impassive, but it makes me happy that she's nervous to discuss it. She should be.

"You know what a good submissive does and how she behaves, don't you? I was under the impression I wouldn't have to teach you that," I say with a frown.

Her eyes lock on mine as she replies. "Yes, Anthony." Her complete attention and obedience is fucking beautiful. And hearing my name on her lips makes my dick jump. I know she has expectations just as much as I do. They'll help us for now, but they can hurt us, too.

"Earlier, you hadn't agreed to be mine. In fact, you said no and chose death at first." Her eyes stay locked on mine, but her mouth stays closed. "Because you weren't aware of my terms, you weren't punished. But now, you're mine. That behavior you displayed will get your ass whipped, kitten."

She nods her head diligently.

"You deliberately teased me." I bring my finger to her mouth and trace her bottom lip. Her mouth parts slightly, but I pull away. "Next time you'll find out what happens when you tempt that side of me." I have to work hard to keep my eyes locked on hers rather than roaming her body and picturing those sweet lips wrapped around my cock. "Do you understand, kitten?"

"Yes, Anthony." A wicked smirk pulls my lips up.

Now that she's agreed, we can really play.

CHAPTER 11

CATHERINE

"**Y**ou need a bath and then dinner, kitten." Anthony rises, towering above me as I sit paralyzed on the sofa.

"Yes, Anthony." The words fall easily from my lips in a tone I've only ever imagined could come from me. I feel... numb. Almost as though I'm not present in my own body. I don't understand how things have changed so quickly. I've gone from being in a dark, cold cell with nothing, to this room that's more beautiful than anything I could ever imagine.

"Come." Anthony holds his hand out for me and I quickly place my hand in his. I'm relying solely on my instincts and what I've read in my romance novels. My heart flutters as he leads me to a set of double doors carved from wood. I want to touch them, but I don't. Not with him here. I imagine he has cameras everywhere, but as soon as he leaves, I want to touch everything. I need to see what all he brought from my home and what he has for me here. A part of me wants to cry with joy and feel nothing but gratitude. But that part of me is fucking stupid.

And I'm not stupid. This is a gilded cage for his pampered pet. And he intends for me to be that pet, his *kitten*. I can play along. I *will* play along. At some point I'll be able to get out of here. I just need to survive and be whatever it is that he wants me to be until that time comes.

He opens the doors and reveals the most gorgeous bathroom I've ever seen.

The walls are lined with a beautiful pale blue paisley wallpaper. Hanging from the center of the ceiling is a silver and Lucite chandelier positioned directly above a large, oval soaking tub. Running the entire length of the back wall is a huge walk-in shower complete with waterfall shower heads and massage jets arranged symmetrically on the walls. There's a large double vanity to the left, and that makes chills prick over my skin. Is he staying here, too? It never occurred to me that he would. This space is feminine and designed for a woman. I try to ignore the fact that there are two sinks and walk forward to the shower.

My heartbeat picks up. I know what he's going to want. I'm not an idiot.

"Kitten." I hear Anthony's rebuke from behind me and I quickly turn around to face him. I don't know what I did wrong. My knees weaken and my immediate reaction is to lower myself to the ground to show complete submission. I don't want to go back to the cell. I can't. I can't go backward.

Before I can drop to the tiled floor, Anthony reaches out and firmly grips my arm and waist. "Now now, you're alright. I just want you to relax." His hands loosen on my waist and I struggle to look at him. I feel lost and powerless.

"I want you to undress out here. I need to take a look at you." I nod my head at his words. Obviously that's what he wanted. He's already made me cum and seen my naughty bits, so this isn't that far of a stretch. But it feels dirty somehow. I guess in a way it's more intimate. I pull the straps off my shoulders and let the thin nightgown fall into a heap around my feet.

Naturally I want to cover myself, but I don't. I've read enough dark romance to know better. A submissive doesn't hide her body from her dom.

Anthony's quiet. He doesn't move to touch me, and he doesn't say anything at all. I find myself growing more anxious the longer he stays silent. What if he doesn't find me attractive? What if he changes his mind? I close my eyes and try to breathe easy, but I can't.

I'm not skinny, but I wouldn't say I'm overweight either. I've got a pear shape and the cellulite on my ass to go with it. My breasts are small, but perky. I think I could be cute if

I wasn't so fucking pale. His eyes don't give anything away. I wish he'd just say something already.

Before I can go into a full panic attack, he reaches out and places his hand on the dip in my waist. He crouches low and puts his face just inches above my pelvis. His fingers trace over a small scar on my hip.

"Where did this come from?" he asks.

I look down at the shiny white scar. It's hardly noticeable. I've had it most of my life and I've never thought twice about it. "When I was younger, I hit something I guess, or fell." I swallow thickly and say, "I don't remember."

He nods his head and walks around my body, looking over every inch. I feel like he's evaluating whether or not he's going to keep me, and I'm terrified he'll find me lacking.

From behind me, I feel his hands gently rest on my hips, and I close my eyes as I feel his hot breath on my shoulder. I gently tilt my neck, expecting him to kiss me there, but he doesn't. In an instant he's gone, and I'm left standing awkwardly as he completes the circle and stands in front of me as though it didn't happen.

For a moment I wonder if he even touched me at all. Maybe I imagined it.

I clear my throat after a moment of silence, but he speaks before I can and says, "You're beautiful. Every inch of you." I look up at him with surprise and wonder. He sounds so sincere. I can't help but believe he really does find me beautiful.

"You're dirty though. Let me clean you." I back away out of instinct as he walks around me toward the shower. My breathing picks up, and I can't hide the fact that I don't want this. I don't want his hands roaming my body for a mix of reasons. He's fucking good at this game, and there's a small piece of me that I know would cave at his touch. I don't trust him. I don't want him to take care of me.

"Would you rather I give you space, kitten?" he asks.

I can't hide my shock. I can hardly believe that he would leave me alone in this room. That's a lot of trust for him to extend to me. I could easily break the glass and use a piece as a weapon. Either on myself or him. As if reading my mind, he cocks a brow.

"You aren't going to make me regret that, are you? You've been so good today. I'd hate for you to upset me just before bedtime." There's a dark threat in his voice, and I'm quick to shake my head and alleviate any worries he has.

"I didn't think you would. You're smarter than that," he says.

"Yes, Anthony." My response earns me a warm smile, and I hate that it eases the apprehension in me, but it does.

"Dinner will be ready in an hour; you'll need to be done by then."

"I'm not very hungry." I speak just above a murmur and stare at the beautiful marble floor. The silence he gives me in return compels me to look at him. He gives me a tight smile.

"I understand not having an appetite, but you need to eat,

kitten." He takes a step back and looks into my eyes. I try to break eye contact, but I can't. The intensity of his gaze has me pinned.

"Tomorrow will be different; you know that, don't you?" he asks with an even voice.

Tomorrow I'm his, and I'll have expectations to meet. I know. I know what this is. Regret overwhelms me. I've read this story so many times. Girl gets taken and held against her will. But this is no story. It's not something I can edit and critique. What's happening right now isn't the same as words on a page that can be changed on a whim.

"It's going to be good, kitten." His calm tone eases the stress threatening to consume me. He grips my chin in between his thumb and forefinger. He leans down with his lips close to mine, but he doesn't let them touch. My body ignites from the proximity of our bodies--mine naked, and his fully clothed. He holds such power over me, yet his touch is gentle. I almost lean into him, expecting him to kiss me, but he doesn't. He whispers, "You're going to love this kitten; I promise you."

I close my eyes, waiting for him to kiss me, but instead he drops his hand and turns to leave me. "Sleep well, kitten," he says as he opens the double doors and leaves me alone.

I watch the doors shut as his body leaves my view. The loud click fills the bathroom and I finally wrap my arms around my body. I feel stunned. Confused. And scared. More than anything, I feel lost.

I turn the water on and let the steam fill the room before I finally get into the shower. The heat feels like absolute heaven on my sore shoulders. I stand under the stream, letting the water hit me as I absorb everything. It takes a long while for me to reach for the soap and and wash the grime of the cell away. When my fingers travel lower, the anger comes along with bitter disappointment. I let him touch me.

I scrub my body harder and turn up the heat. The reality of the situation makes my breathing become ragged.

I close my eyes as the tears leak out and lean my body against the cool tiled wall. I slowly slide down until I'm on my ass and holding my knees to my chest.

I don't know how I'll ever get out of here. But I will.

Part of me thinks I should be grateful. The fucking psycho who took me is at least giving me space and letting me stay in a beautiful prison. It could be worse. But it's still a prison. And I don't deserve this. *It's better than death.* I can't deny that. I'm safe for now. Or at least I've been given the impression of safety.

I'll obey him to save myself from punishment, but I can't forget what's really going on here.

I can't let him break me. I can't let him win.

The first chance I'm given, I'm running and never looking back.

It takes me an hour before I finally go back to the bedroom. I stop in my tracks when I see a tray on the end of the bed.

I walk closer to it with disbelief. Sitting on the tray is a sage green teacup with the corresponding saucer on top to keep the heat in. And next to it are two melatonin pills.

I reach down and slowly move the saucer; the steam spills out beautifully from the freshly steeped chamomile tea.

He was watching. I already knew that though. I knew he would be watching me.

I've read countless books where the heroine is taken and forced to submit. I pick the teacup up and put it to my lips. I close my eyes as I take a sip and sit down on the bed. I look around the bedroom, the one he designed with me in mind, and think back to all those dark romances.

I've already read this story, but this is different. The way this story ends is entirely up to me and my choices from here on out.

CHAPTER 12

ANTHONY

I pull the covers closer around me. I do it every night as though they'll protect me, but they won't. No one can protect me. This is something that has to happen. I ruined her life. When she had me, everything changed. She's hurting because of me. Dad's never nice to her anymore. He always makes her cry now. When he hits her, she hits me. It's only fair, she says. I deserve it. I should never have been born.

I hear the door creak open and shut behind her. I know it's coming. The belt comes down hard and I cry out as little as possible. I hear her, but I ignore it. I feel the pain, but I pretend I'm numb. I think about Tommy. As long as she stays here, he's safe. He didn't do anything. It's not his fault. It's my fault. I try *to be good and stay quiet, but the belt whips through the air and smacks across my face. I can't help that I screamed.*

I can't help it. I hear them coming. No! I shake my head as she shoves the belt under the covers. My heart beats faster. I tried to be good. I tried. Please forgive me.

My eyes slowly open and and my body seems frozen. It takes a moment for my heart to calm. I'm used to this. Everything will be fine. It's nothing that matters anymore. My racing heart is the only indication that I've had that fucking nightmare again. I clear my throat and get my shit together. I do my best to feel nothing, and for the most part that's true.

I don't feel a god damned thing reliving that memory.

I look over to my alarm and move the switch before the clock has a chance to display 6:00 AM and go off. I can't remember the last time the alarm actually had a chance to go off. It doesn't matter though, as long as I'm up to start the day.

I check my phone again. Vince still hasn't written me back.

I look at the last message he sent me. It reads, *1 month.* I have one month with her until the Cassanos want proof that she's dead.

One month, my ass. I'm not giving her up in a month. No fucking way. I've only just gotten my hands on her.

I calm myself by thinking about how she's safe here.

Having her in her room soothes the beast inside of me. My kitten is where she belongs, and she's adjusting well.

She cried for nearly an hour last night. I hated watching her break down like that. It's only natural though. And now that it's out of her system, she's taken to her surroundings well. She checked everywhere for an escape though. I chuckle as I make my way to the monitors in the closet.

Her alarm is going to go off at 7 a.m., and she's still curled up in bed. I imagine she's going to want to fight me on this one. She's used to getting up at 8 a.m. I'd be happy to let her have the extra hour, if she asks. I may prime her to ask for permission so she can see that I'm willing to adjust for her. But I'm not sure she'll bring it up and risk going back to the cell. She might be afraid that even just asking me will displease me. Her fear is a big part of what's holding us back. I just need to give her time and let that dissipate.

I watch her sleeping peacefully and something inside of me seems to shift into place. I know everything is going to work out perfectly. Every ounce of worry leaves me.

I walk with purpose to the bathroom and go about my daily ritual. I look at my reflection in the mirror and run my hand over the stubble on my jaw. I need to get myself together before I go to her. And she should be doing the same for me. She isn't though.

I cluck my tongue before pulling out the razor and shaving cream.

I'm happy about that. This will be a perfect training opportunity. I asked her if she needed me to explain what being a submissive means, and she said no. She was wrong. Obviously my little kitten missed some vital information in her books. She should always be presentable for me. I can't wait to show her what happens when she doesn't meet my expectations. My kitten's in for a treat.

As I rinse the razor in a hot stream of water, my phone pings. I close my eyes with frustration.

I've told them I'm taking some time off, but Tommy insists I'm needed. I'd do anything for my brother, but sometimes he gets on my fucking nerves.

I text him back that I'll meet him later tonight. I just want to enjoy this, but instead I feel tense. It's because I know they're going to take her from me.

They can't.

He said I could have this.

He gave me his word.

I don't give a fuck about the business that we get from the Cassanos, or what their expectations were. I bought her, so she's mine to do whatever I fucking want with her.

And right now, I want to get information from her, whip her ass for not being ready and then have her writhing beneath me.

My shoulders loosen up and I let out an easy breath as my dick springs to life. Maybe if I just keep all the blood in my cock I won't get so fucking worked up over Vince and his lack of a god damned backbone.

I splash some water on my face and pat it dry. I'm only in pajama pants that are hanging low on my hips, and my erection is obvious. That's good though. I want her to know how much I want her.

I look back in the mirror and breathe easy.

It's only me and her right now.

Time to play with my kitten.

CHAPTER 13

CATHERINE

I wake up with a shriek ripped from my throat as a hard hand smacks against my ass.

I bolt upright from the bed and grab the covers, pulling them close to my body as I stare wide-eyed at Anthony. My heart beats rapidly with fear, but then is replaced by something else entirely. The brief dread that I feel fucking vanishes.

Holy fuck, he looks like he came straight off the cover of my favorite smutty novels. That chiseled "V" at his hips and his hard and lean muscular body are exactly what I've longed to wake up to. Except that he just spanked me, and he's looking at me like I kicked his puppy.

I have no fucking clue what I did to piss him off. I slowly

move into a submissive position, watching him cautiously. But his eyes aren't on me. They're on my ass and probably admiring the bright red mark he left.

"Nice of you to wake up." He finally gives me a clue as to what I did wrong. His tone is playful and it eases a small part of me, but I can't forget. This is an illusion and a game to him. I can't relax; I need to keep my guard up. I pull at the hem of the nightgown I'm wearing. It's the longest one I found in the dresser, but it still shows far too much of my ass.

My eyes home in on the clock on the nightstand, but I can't see the time. I vaguely remember smacking that annoying fucker when the alarm woke me up earlier. My heart sinks, and my stomach drops with fear. Day one, and already I've fucked this up. I didn't fucking know, although I should have.

"What do you have to say for yourself?" he asks with a heated stare.

I'm fucking exhausted because a psycho took me from my home and said psycho happens to get up earlier than I do. Add that to the list of things that make you a prick.

I clear my throat as softly as possible and decide to apologize. I can't risk getting in even more trouble right now. I can't go back to the cell. I remember how nice he was last night, I just need to appeal to that side of him. "I'm sorry, Anthony. I didn't realize."

"You're supposed to be presentable for me." His voice is stern.

I keep my eyes on his as my breathing picks up. He's right,

I should've known that. It's not like I thought I could sleep in and lounge around all day.

"I wasn't sure when you'd be here," I say as softly as my voice allows.

"You should *always* be ready." He walks to the nightstand and picks up the clock, holding it out for me to see. "But this should give you a pretty good fucking clue as to when I'll be here."

A yawn creeps up on me and I really do try to hold it in. But I can't stop myself, and I literally let out a huge yawn as he's reprimanding me. I cover my mouth with my hand and shake my head. "I'm sorry, I didn't--"

"You didn't what?" he asks with a hard edge. His eyes narrow as he sets the clock down with more grace and care than is needed. I can tell he's trying to hold in his anger. A darkness I haven't seen yet gathers around him. Fuck, this isn't good.

"I'm sorry, Anthony. I didn't mean to upset you." Fear heats my blood as I scoot backward on the bed. "I didn't mean to yawn. It just slipped out, and I didn't know about the time."

"You seem to have relaxed a little too much, kitten. Did you forget who you are?" he asks. His words send chills down my spine and strike fear into my heart.

I don't know how to respond; my mouth opens, but words don't come out. I don't know what he wants me to say. He puts his knee on the bed and reaches out, grabbing my ankle and dragging me across the bed. The nightgown travels up my body and I desperately try to keep it down. But I don't struggle against his hold, and I don't fight him. I let him drag me over to him.

"Mine. That's who you are. You. Are. *Mine*." His anger wanes as I look back at him. He commands me in a calmer tone. "Say it."

I hold his gaze and answer quickly. "Yours. I'm yours." His chest rises and falls with his steadying breath. My pussy clenches as I see how my words have tamed him somewhat. I love the power I have over him, but I'm not a fool, and this isn't right. It's wrong. What I feel for him, this entire situation--it's all wrong.

He's still trying to calm himself down and I know I need to say something to make him less angry with me. "I will be pres--present--" I try to tell him I'll be ready for him at all times. But I stumble over the words. Although he hasn't hit me, I'm scared to death he will. Or worse, that he'll throw me back into the cell and leave me there.

"Shh." His hand cups my chin and he looks me in the eyes. "You will be presentable for me by 8 a.m. every morning. Unless that's too early for you?" He cocks his head at me, daring me to disagree.

I swallow the lump in my throat and nod my head. "Yes, Anthony." He looks back at me like he's waiting for more. But I don't know what he wants me to say.

After a moment he asks, "Have you disobeyed me?"

I shake my head no. My breathing becomes erratic as I wonder if I've defied him unintentionally. "I didn't mean to. Not on purpose."

"I know you haven't. But you also haven't been a very good pet, have you?"

"I'm sorry. I'll be better." I don't want to go back to the cell. I can't go back there. My heart begins to thump painfully in my chest as I imagine being imprisoned there again. I'll be better for him. I know I can be better.

"You need to try harder, or this will never work." I search his eyes for sympathy or understanding, but I see nothing. He doesn't wait for me to speak as he continues.

"Right now, for instance. You're hesitating to answer me. You aren't speaking to me. You aren't ready." I draw in a short breath at the no-nonsense list of shit I've done to displease him already. The worst part is that I really should know better. I've read dozens or more books about submissives and dominants. I know all about power exchanges--fuck, I've fantasized about it. And yet here I am. Failing at it. Failing at being a submissive pet like I've dreamt about.

"I don't like that," he says quietly. Fear grips my heart as I register his words. I can do this. I can be better. I need to be better so he keeps me. At least until I can get the fuck out of here. "I'm going to punish you for it."

I start to shake my head; my body feels paralyzed. It was

just one mistake. I can fix it. "Please don't send me back--"

"No, kitten," he says as he strokes my cheek and looks me square in the eyes. I instantly close my eyes and hold my breath. "Not a punishment for disobeying me." He gently pulls me by the hands into a seated position and pets my hair. "The kind of punishment that will push your limits and end with both of us being satisfied." His anger completely vanishes as he gives me a small smirk and says, "You know the type of punishment I'm talking about."

Everything in my body relaxes as I nod back and reply, "Yes." I know what he means, and the thought makes my blood race. I have to break his gaze as a blush comes over me and my core heats. What the fuck is wrong with me?

A low chuckle rises in his chest.

"Now that you're here, kitten, it's time to really start playing." I look anywhere but his eyes and end up staring right at the erection in his pants. Oh, fuck, another wave of arousal hits me. I close my eyes and try to ignore it. This is just pretend. This is something I need to get through until I can escape.

I feel the bed dip, and I know he's sitting next to me. I slowly open my eyes as he speaks. "Time to be a good pet and take your punishment, kitten." I want to ask him why he's doing this. I want to ask him to just let me go. But a darker side of me wants to be punished. I want to feel the pain turn to pleasure, just like I've read about before. I want those scenes to come to life. I crawl on my knees and move to drape my body over his lap with my hips atop his thighs. I know that I have this coming. I have to be better next time. It'll be easy. I've read so many god damned books so I should fucking ace this.

I think about them as he slips my gown up to my waist. I'm not wearing any underwear because he simply didn't provide me with any. My heart sputters in my chest as his hand caresses one of my ass cheeks and then the other. My body is stiff and I keep waiting for the smack every time I feel his hand lift up, but he just continues to massage my ass, drawing out my punishment. I turn my head to the side and just breathe. My shoulders ease lower and I close my eyes, enjoying his touch.

He positions me across his lap and places one of his legs over mine. My eyes open, and I know it's coming. A hand gentles on my ass and then lifts before landing hard with a loud *smack*!

"Fuck!" I yell out, and resist trying to move away. My eyes scrunch as another hard, stinging smack lands on my right cheek and then again on my left. I ball my hands into fists and close my eyes tightly as the stinging makes my eyes water. My throat closes, and I can't help that I flinch at the next smack. Tears leak from my eyes. Fuck, it hurts. Fucking hell. I cover my face with my hands as another hard smack lands on my ass and forces a scream from me.

I prepare for another blow, but it doesn't come. He rubs my tender ass and whispers, "You're close, kitten. So close." My ass feels so fucking hot and so damn sore that even the faintest soothing touch stings. He lifts his hand and brings it down over the crack of my ass. His fingertips barely touch my pussy. I try to arch my back as a warmth stirs in my belly. I shake my head as he continues my spanking. Soon the stinging pain turns into a numbing sensation, and the numbness is replaced by something else. Something hot and delightful that makes my core clench.

I groan into the sheets as his hand slaps my tender skin repeatedly. He pauses to rub my ass, and I find myself moving against him.

"Stay still, kitten," he says as a warning. His fingers dip between the folds of my pussy.

"Yes, Anthony." The words fall from my lips with lust. He raises his hand, and another hard spank greets my ass. "Uhh!" I scream out as my body bows. I've never felt this before, this heated need for more. I writhe under him, but then remember his command.

Still.

I force myself to remain motionless as more blows rain down on my ass. Right, left, center. Over and over again. Each time he hits the center, his fingers sink lower.

The pain morphs into something entirely different and I feel myself rise higher and higher. My head thrashes as I try to resist, but my body betrays me. I'm fucking soaking wet for him. After a few more hard swats, he stops and leans down, planting a kiss on my left ass cheek.

"What do you say, kitten?" he asks as his hands gently caress my ass.

I have no fucking clue what he's talking about. My heart beats faster with the desire of wanting to answer him correctly. And then it hits me.

"Thank you for my punishment," I say just above a murmur.

His fingers travel down my ass and over my puckered hole. My lungs stop as his fingertips hover there. They prod slightly, but only for a moment. Then they travel lower and dig into my heat. The feeling is so unexpected, and so shockingly needed.

I grind on his hand as his fingers pump in and out of me. I moan into the sheets shamelessly. He pulls them out, only to move the moisture to my clit and circle it with no mercy. My back stiffens and my body tingles as every part of me is on edge. And then he pinches my hardened nub and I shatter. I fall off the edge and break, with waves of pleasure controlling every inch of my body. It's a paralyzing release that leaves me breathless.

It's quiet for a long moment as I lie limp across his lap. Finally he breaks the silence. "Good job, kitten. You did really well. I'm proud of you." For some reason his praise makes my heart swell. I quickly look away and try to ignore the warmth I feel in my chest. Not to mention his fucking erection digging into my stomach.

He reaches over me to grab something off the nightstand, but I don't see what it is. I hear a cap snap open and I hiss as a cool dab of cream lands on one ass cheek and then the other. He chuckles, and it's the sexiest fucking sound I've ever heard. He gently rubs the cream into my skin and I practically purr with affection. *Aftercare.* A small smile plays at my lips, but then I remember everything. Shame replaces every good feeling. I swallow as spikes seem to grow in my throat. *What the fuck just happened?*

He reaches over to the nightstand for something else, and this time I look. My brow furrows as I catch a glimpse of something that I'm almost positive is a syringe.

He stabs the needle into my ass, making me wince before I can do a damn thing about it. After a second he pulls it out and rubs the tender spot. "There kitten, now you've had your shots."

I look at him from the corner of my eye as he lifts me off his lap to sit next to him. Fuck, my ass hurts! I'm too scared to ask what the shot was, but I can't take my eyes off of it. I need to know what he's putting into my body. I swallow thickly and bite out the words.

"Anthony, what was that?"

"A shot of Depo-Provera," he answers confidently.

Birth control.

He sits me upright, making me cringe from the stinging sensation and moves off the bed. I keep my head lowered and try not to show how fucking worried I am.

"I'll be back in one hour. Be ready for me this time." He cups my chin in his hand. "I've been going easy on you, so don't make me regret that."

His lips hover an inch away from mine, but he doesn't lean in. My breathing picks up and I wait for him to kiss me. But he doesn't.

He drops his hand and walks quickly to the door.

"One hour. Don't disappoint me, kitten."

CHAPTER 14

CATHERINE

I breathe in deep and look at my reflection as I layer on one more coat of mascara. The cabinet is filled with high-end beauty products that are all brand new. It also contains my makeup bag, which he obviously stole from my house.

I've been watching the clock like a hawk.

My hair's tied back in a loose braid, and my makeup is clean and natural-looking, just enough to cover the imperfections.

The closet is stuffed with all sorts of clothing. From cocktail dresses, to slutty role-playing costumes, to everyday pieces that I actually love. He also brought along a duffel bag packed with a few items that I wear all the time.

The variety of clothing, makeup, and accessories is

strangely familiar. Some things I recognize as mine, but the new additions are all nicer, more luxurious versions of what I already own.

The one thing he didn't grab were the owl earrings my mother left me.

They were hers, and when she found out she only had three months left to live, she gave them to me.

They're gorgeous. I'd admired them since I was a little girl. The earrings are yellow gold with ruby flowers in the centers of the owls, but I've never worn them. I was always too afraid I'd lose them. And now they're gone.

I tilt my head back and exhale, waving my hands around my face to cool my eyes and keep me from crying. It's almost time, and I can't ruin my makeup and piss him off.

I don't know why I was so lackadaisical when he came in this morning. Maybe it's because I slept so damn well. It took forever to actually get to sleep, but when I did, I slept wonderfully. I guess allowing myself to cry some helped. I'm not sure why I wasn't more alert this morning. Maybe it's because he was so lenient last night, but whatever the reason, I can't let it happen again.

I calm myself down and put the mascara back. Everything's neat and put away. It makes me feel at ease. I just need to make the bed and then I can wait for him.

I always make my bed in the morning. I think staying at home all day has made me a tidier person than I ever was before.

So long as I'm capable of making the bed, I'm able to do anything. I snort a humorless laugh as I move the sheets into place and reach for the duvet. It's so pretty and soft. It's off-white, with thin silver threading making a paisley design throughout.

I bend at the waist to lay my head down on the bed and love how I sink in to the mattress and smell the comforting scent of fresh laundry. As I inhale deeply, I hear the doorknob turn and the door slowly open. I quickly climb the bed and kneel at the end of it. I don't know if this is where he wants me. My heart races. I don't know any of his preferences. He never told me. He may want my hair a certain way, my makeup to be heavier, or my clothes to be different. I have no fucking clue. I need to ask him. He hasn't given me anything. He's not playing fair.

As soon as I find out what kind of mood he's in, I'm asking. So long as it's a good mood.

I hear him walk by the sofa and toward the bed, but I don't look up. I keep my head bowed and wait. I'm on my knees, sitting back on my heels with my hands slightly in front of me, palms up.

I've read a lot of books and there are so many damn positions. I don't know which one he means by kneel. For Christ's sake, in movies they kneel on one foot, but I'm sure he doesn't mean that though.

I watch as he picks up my hand and places it gently on my thigh and does the same with the other. His fingers tilt my chin up so I have to look at him.

"No need to bow, kitten." He pets my hair as he talks. It's soothing and rhythmic. "I want your eyes on me always. You never have to look away."

"Yes, Anthony." I feel like I'm playing a role. It gives me a small thrill, but I have to remember this is an act. All of this is an act.

"Did you find everything you need?" he asks.

I look up at him through my lashes. He's so fucking handsome. It still amazes me that he felt the need to take a woman when he could have anyone he wanted. That a man like him would stoop this low. I realize I haven't answered his question and bite my lip. I want to tell him I want more of my things, but I can't. I'm too scared to do anything to upset him. Because of that, I merely nod my head in assent.

"So I packed everything that you need, then?" he asks with slight disbelief in his tone. The way he says it makes me feel like I'd be a liar now to tell him that I want more of my things. My skin heats and I feel nauseated. I feel trapped in a corner, like no matter what I do, it'll be wrong.

"Kitten," he says as he leans my body against his chest and runs soothing strokes along my back.

"You can tell me anything. I promise I won't get mad," he says.

"I want to go home." The words fall out easily. As though they've been perched there, waiting for me to release them.

"I know you do, but you can't." He keeps petting my back and I hate him for it. I want to move out of his embrace, but at the same time I don't. I need the comfort.

"What else did you want to ask?" he says. I'm quiet for a moment and he adds, "If you want certain things, you'll need to ask for them."

"I have other things I want," I say softly into his chest. I wait with bated breath for his reaction.

"We'll go together. Later tonight." His answer surprises me so much I go completely still. I'm afraid if I move, or if I even breathe, he'll change his mind.

"I want you to be happy here. You know that, don't you?" he asks.

"Yes, Anthony." I respond with the only answer that seems fit, but really, I don't know that to be true. He wants me here to serve him. To play his fucked up game. He doesn't want me here to be happy. He's not doing me any god damned favors.

He finally releases me and I maintain my position.

He looks me over, assessing me before taking me by my hand.

"It's time for breakfast, kitten." He leads me off the bed and to the door. We're leaving the room. Hope rises in my chest. I wait for the sash, but he doesn't pull it out. Maybe he'll let his guard down today, and I'll have a chance to run.

He looks back at me as he enters in the code. I bite my bottom lip and look away. Damn it. He grunts a laugh and it pisses me off. At the click he opens the door and reaches out to prop it open with his foot. I consider grabbing the door, swinging it open and running. My heart beats fast and adrenaline rushes through my blood at the thought. But I don't do it. I watch as he wheels in a steel cart and the door slowly closes. My eyes fall to the ground and I feel like a fucking coward.

"Now now, kitten, stop that." I look up at my captor, at my dom, with sad eyes.

"I just want to go home." I say the words again and I'm sure I sound pathetic.

"You are home," he says absolutely. It crushes something inside me and I have to work hard not to cry. I stand there while he wheels the cart over to the sofa and sets up covered dishes on the coffee table. I look between him and the locked door.

It could be so much worse. He was supposed to kill me. I close my eyes and steady my breathing as I consider how many other ways this could have gone. I just need to behave. He can't keep me here forever.

"Come, kitten." My feet move toward him before I'm even fully conscious of his command.

I start to sit on the sofa, but he holds his hand up and I freeze.

"On your knees," he says.

I only hesitate a fraction of a second before gracefully sitting on my heels. I put my hands on my thighs where he placed them earlier. I can do this. I know I can. And I can win his trust and I can get the fuck out of here. I just need to role-play. I can do it. I know I can.

"Let's play a game, kitten." He starts talking and I give him my full attention, but I don't want to play a game. I want to go home. I want to read my books, talk to my clients, and engage with my group of readers on social media. Every hour I'm away from them kills the interaction rates. It's fucking horrible for business. I breathe in deeply. My books and my work are my life. And he's murdering both of them right now.

"Between every bite we'll ask each other a question." He lifts a silver dome off of a plate and a delicious scent fills my lungs. I inhale deeply, loving the smell of peppers and sausage and eggs. I eye the dish. Omelets. My mouth waters. "Does that sound like fun to you?" he asks.

No, I think, but of course I answer, "Yes."

"Does it really?" he asks, immediately countering my simple answer.

"Fun? No, it doesn't. But it sounds like something to do," I answer honestly out of instinct. I don't have time to be nervous about it. He barks a laugh at my answer and lays a gentle hand on my hair.

"Thank you, kitten." He leans down and plants a kiss in my hair and strokes me gently. It's soothing, and I hate how comforting it is.

I look his body over as he moves to cut a piece of the omelet. I still don't understand why a man like him would do this. I want to ask him. But I'm not going there. I think I'll stick to, *What's the weather like outside, since I can't fucking see it?*

"I'll go first, kitten," he says as he stabs a piece of the egg and puts the fork in front of my mouth. I obediently open and wait for his question. "I know what happened with the Cassanos. But I want you to tell me what you saw." I chew the food slowly as my blood chills. I don't want to talk about it. I also don't know if this is a test. Maybe he really does work for them. Maybe this is all a ploy of some sort. Anxiety creeps up on me. As if reading my mind, he reassures me.

"It's not a trick. I'm just curious how it happened." He sets the fork down as I swallow.

"Would it help if I tell you what I know?" he asks. I nod my head, still unable to speak. Everything that happened fucking destroyed me. I may have been a sweet, shy, book-loving nerd before, but at least I was strong and confident. Going through that shit robbed me of that. I don't want to go back to that fucked up place.

"You saw three of their soldiers kill Judge Hawthort. He was killed by Michael Davis, and Joseph and Brandon Becker. And later you were able to identify them all as well as account for their missing kilos of dope," he says.

I shake my head no and say, "He was alive. I'm fairly sure he was alive." I didn't testify that I saw him dead, and I'm confident that he was alive at the time that I witnessed everything. His body was never found though. It's a very real possibility that he's dead simply because I saw them. Talking about this triggers the memory. I see the hammers in their hands and hear the sound of Brandon smashing his against the judge's knee. He was alive. I hear his screams echo in my head. The bricks and the bags are there. My body turns to ice.

He holds another bite to my lips; my appetite is gone, but I take it. "What else did you see?" he asks.

"Nothing. I never saw anything else," I say.

"They were charged with more," he points out.

"Nothing that I testified to," I answer quickly.

"But you testified to attempted rape and kidnapping?" he asks.

I look away and nod.

"I have another question for you and then I'll lighten it up, kitten." My eyes fall. I don't want another question. This game fucking blows. "I want you to be honest."

I wait nervously for his question.

"Did they touch you?" I know what he's getting at.

I shake my head no. "They tried," I answer, looking to the floor. "That's when I left." Not a single one of them did. Not even Lorenzo. He was having too much fun beating me for sport.

"What about your boyfriend?" he asks. I fucking hate that I ever called him that. Lorenzo helped me escape the pain of losing my mother. He made me feel free and wild. And then he destroyed me. I shake my head no, and I don't realize until

Anthony says something, but my hand moves to my cheek.

"He hit you?" I lock my eyes on Anthony's. His voice is calm. He's been calm the entire time. But his eyes spark with a darkness I never want to see directed at me. I give one curt nod in response. I'm ashamed that I let Lorenzo hurt me. I'm ashamed that it all ever happened.

He scoops a piece of omelet onto the fork and holds it out for me.

I take it simply to fill my mouth so I don't have to talk.

"Your turn, kitten. Ask me anything."

CHAPTER 15

CATHERINE

I can ask him anything at all. Anything I want. "Why me?" I ask simply. I want to know what I did that put a target on my back.

"Well. I told you I was supposed to kill you," he says. The reminder makes my stomach churn. "You were on my list, and like everyone on my list, I did a little digging. In your case, I liked what I found." He spears a small piece of pepper and puts it to my lips.

"Have you...done this before?" I ask before accepting the bite. I fucking hope the answer is no. If it's yes, I know what my next question will be, but I'm afraid of the answer. *Did you kill them when you were done with them?*

"I've played before, but it was only play. You're the first real submissive I've had. And the first complete 24/7 power exchange."

I don't know why, but I hate that there were others before me.

"What happened to them?" I ask before receiving another bite.

"We weren't a good fit," he answers without looking at me. It's the first time he's done that, and I don't like it.

"What did you do to them?" I ask before I can think twice.

He cocks a brow at me. "You mean, did I kill them?" he asks.

My throat closes as I answer in a choked voice, "Yes."

"No, kitten. I didn't kill them." He doesn't answer my unspoken question. *If we don't fit, will he kill me?* He holds another piece out for me to take. But I shake my head. I'm not hungry. The thought of eating another bite makes me sick to my stomach. Of course he will. I'm already supposed to be dead. If we don't fit, or once he's done with me, I'll be dead.

Tears prick my eyes, but I push them back. I need to be good. I need to be fucking perfect until I can get out of here. And the first chance I get, I need to run as fast as I can. I can never stop running. Never.

His strong arms wrap around me as he picks me up and pulls me into his lap to lean against his chest. "I chose you for a reason, kitten." He gently strokes my back and I concentrate on how good it feels to distract myself from the pain. He kisses my hair and then pets me as I lay my head flat against his hard, hot body. I hear his heart beating as he speaks. "You fit me, and this is exactly what I wanted. *You* are exactly what I want."

For now. I focus on the plan. Survive until I'm given an opportunity. I'll be as perfect as I can be. I'll make him want to keep me. I pull back and he readjusts me so I'm sitting in his lap.

I don't know what to say to move past this, but I really just want to move forward and forget that this breakdown ever happened.

"Do you like your new home?" he asks. I'm grateful to discuss a more casual topic, but I can't forget that the fact he's even asking me that question is fucked up. I didn't need a new home. I loved my cabin, and I want to go back.

I glance around the room again. It's as perfect as a gilded cage can be. "Yes, it's beautiful."

"Do you have everything that you need?" he asks.

"There are a few things I'd like to get," I say quietly.

"Yes, you told me that. Other than a few trinkets, is there anything important that I've forgotten?" I feel like he already knows the answer to his question. Like this is a test.

What's the one thing I need here? One thing he hasn't given me is my laptop. I'm afraid to ask for it. It'd be stupid to ask. There's no way he'd let me go online.

He reaches past me to the cart and my mouth drops open.

"I told you earlier, you only need to ask," he says.

I stare at my laptop in his hands. My fucking life is on there. I reach out to take it, expecting him to snatch it away, but he doesn't. Instead he kisses my hair and gently rubs my back. I hug it to my chest and wait for the other shoe to drop.

"Go ahead. I know you have work to do." I swallow the lump in my throat and slowly open my MacBook Pro. It's ten years old. I got it in college. It's really past time to get a new one, but I fucking love my baby.

I type in my password, and the same screen pops up that's greeted me every morning for the last year. It's a meme that says, "You can't read all day, if you don't start in the morning!" I can't help my smile. I instinctively look to check the internet connection. I have a few books loaded on here that I need to put on my Kindle, but what I really need to do is catch up with my FB group and my blogs, plus the editor for my column. I also need to check my email, my website for beta readers, my Goodreads account, and the reading groups online. I take a deep breath and click on my web browser and then hold my breath and stiffen as the screen pops up. I quickly hit exit and look back to Anthony self-consciously.

"Go ahead, kitten. I want to watch you work." I release a breath I didn't know I was holding and look back at Anthony with disbelief.

"I told you I'd give you your life back. I'm a man of my word." I search his eyes for anything but sincerity, but that's all I see. I bite my lip and look back to the computer.

I have work to do, and this is going to take me fucking forever. I shift in his lap. This isn't going to work, but I don't want to push my luck.

"You typically write on your bed, don't you?" he asks.

A chill runs through me at the reminder that he watched me before taking me. "I do."

"Go ahead. I'll sit here. I have a book I'd like to read." It takes a moment for his words to sink in, but when they do, I take my chances and get my ass up and move to the bed with my laptop. I keep my eyes on him as I put the pillow against the headboard for support, and another on my lap for the computer. I've always typed this way. I imagine I always will. It's a bad habit to break.

I watch as Anthony rises and walks to the bookshelf, choosing a paperback and lying down on the sofa. He crosses his ankles and it's the sexiest sight I've ever seen.

It's fucking unreal that he's letting me get online.

Something's up though. And I don't fucking like it. Everything is a test. Every last fucking thing. My eyes stay on him as I type in my password. My email is slow to open, but it does. I click on my emails one at a time and type my responses, but I keep looking back to Anthony. He simply turns a page, appearing fully engrossed in his reading.

I feel so fucking uneasy. He's not at all what I expected, and the thought that I'd be able to do this is just...insane. He's fucking insane. Not just mentally unstable, but certifiably

insane if he thinks I'm not going to message someone--
anyone--that I've been taken. I don't give a fuck that he's been
nice, or that he's hot, or that this is literally a fucking dark
dream come true for me. There's no way I'm not going to try
to get the hell out of here.

I click on a new tab and bring up Facebook. Cheryl's my
personal assistant and my go-to gal for everything. My cursor
hovers over the box to message her, but she's already sent me
five messages. The third one was her freaking out that I didn't
respond at all yesterday, but the fourth and fifth are her fixing
my shit and wishing me well because she refuses to believe
that I'm dead and I better fucking message her back or she'll
find me and kill me. Yeah, that's Cheryl.

I type in a lame excuse and don't mention shit. Yet. I
want to. Every fucking voice inside of me is screaming to do
something and tell someone. But I'd be stupid to think I'd get
away with it, right? I watch Anthony for a minute as I copy
and paste an email to send to another reader.

What would he do to me if I did? Kill me. The answer
is obvious, but he hasn't hurt me yet. My ass smarts at the
thought. It still fucking hurts, although the cream he rubbed
in did wonders for the worst of the pain. I don't know where
I am. I'm not sure that there's any way they'd find me.

*Hey, Cheryl. Some psycho took me, I'm not sure where.
Could you figure out a way for someone to rescue me?*

Yeah...that's not going to fucking work. My heart races

and my fingers itch to type something, *anything* to help me get the fuck out of here.

I will be good. I will not email the police and post all over social media that I've been kidnapped. 'Cause that would be fucking obvious. But I could sure as fuck sneak in some clues.

I type in, *Busy with Comfort Food*, hoping she'll catch on. It's a classic book where the heroine is kidnapped. I hope she understands and catches the subtlety. Maybe she can help me. She can relay information for me, and I can figure out where the fuck I am.

She instantly replies, *Whatcha eating?*

Jesus, Cheryl. I barely keep myself from rolling my eyes. As I consider what to type next, Anthony's phone pings in his pocket. He takes it out and looks at it and then right at me. My heart stops. But he merely gives me a tight smile and goes back to his book.

I can't help but think that message was about me. That I'd been caught. My skin prickles with goosebumps and my hands shake. What would he do if he caught me? What good would it do for people to know I'd been taken if they had no way to find me? It takes me a moment, but I'm finally able to type back, *Omelets, brb.*

No more of that shit. I go back to checking all of my notifications. I post a few memes, along with a fun pic of a hot man with a question for the readers to answer about Linda's new book release. I download four betas to my Kindle as I message three authors that I'm a day behind. The hours tick by as I make small dents in my work.

I only look up when I see Anthony rise and stretch. I hold my breath and wait for him as he strides toward me.

"I'll be back, kitten." He leans down and looks over my computer for only a second and then gives me a smile. I feel that sexual tension between us, the need to lean forward and kiss him.

But instead his brows furrow and he looks back at the screen, reading over the posts in my group. After a moment he breaks the silence. "I wonder what your group would suggest, kitten," he says, taking a seat next to me. His arm wraps around my waist. Like this is normal, like we're a couple.

"Ask them this." It's a command.

I click the box and prepare to type in a question. My heart beats chaotically in my chest as he tells me what to write. "What would you do if you woke up in a basement and a man gave you two choices: die, or be his?" I type in his words and hover over the submit button. It's fucking insane that he's having me ask them. But it's also a common thing I do. I pose a question by picking a scenario from a common trope to engage them. I already know what most will answer.

I hit enter, and it doesn't take long for them to start commenting. They love these questions, and frankly, so do I. But not this one. Because this is real.

"Well, your friends have some good ideas as to what you

should be doing." I consider pointing out the comment from a reader about gouging his eyes out, but I don't.

I read down the list of responses. Nearly forty comments already. Most say the same thing.

Be his!

I choose the second option!

Well, if he's hot--that's a no brainer!

All their responses seem so natural online. They're meant for humor, and to be cheeky replies. A week ago, I would have said the same. But it's not *real*. You wouldn't really do that. It's not that easy. I want to yell at Anthony. I'm pissed that he would do that shit to me, that he would make me feel like I'm the one holding back.

"Given that the choice is to die or to be his, it's clearly a given." I read the words flatly. It's one of the comments, but also the truth. I keep my voice even and my eyes on the screen.

I can feel Anthony's eyes on me, and I regret opening my mouth at all. I can't look at him, so I stare at the screen. The comments continue coming in.

Agree to be his...duh! lol

Well I wouldn't make it easy for him...

Agree! It could be hot as hell ;)

I close the laptop and try to swallow the lump growing in my throat. I can't read them. I hate the ease at which the replies come in. Normally I love them. I love my group of readers and authors. But right now I can't stand how easy they make giving in sound. Anthony pulls the laptop from me and cradles me in his lap.

"I just wanted you to see why it was easy to pick you." His voice is gentle and it vibrates up his chest. I lean deeper into him. "You're primed to enjoy this because deep down you know how good this can be."

I shake my head against his broad shoulders. Those are fantasies.

He grips my chin in his hand and leans into me. Our lips are closer than they have ever been before. "Real life and fantasy can blur, kitten. This can be whatever you want it to be."

My heart aches in my chest. *Be his.* How easy it seems to give in.

And I do. A piece of my armor cracks enough that I lean into his embrace and brush my lips against his. He doesn't kiss back, not at first. And it kills something deep down inside of me. Before I can pull away, his hands grip my hips and he pushes me down onto the bed and kisses me with passion. His erection rubs against my clit and he rocks against me as our tongues meet and our kiss turns into something more. I feel my walls falling down around me. It would be so easy to give in to him. To live something I've only ever thought would be a dream.

Just as the word touches my tongue, *please*, he pulls back and stands, leaving me panting and lost in lust. I slowly push myself into a sitting position as he climbs off the bed and gives me a heated glare. I know he wants me. I would have begged him though.

I close my eyes and turn back to my computer. A moment of silence passes. I fucking would have begged him. I was going to do it. What the ever loving fuck is wrong with me?

"Time's up, kitten," he says, reaching for the laptop.

"I need to work." I speak without thinking. His eyes narrow and I reword my plea. "I'm really far behind. Please, Anthony." I sound so pathetic and weak. I hate it. *I'm so fucking weak.*

"You can download the books and write your articles without going online," he answers, and he's partly right, but he's fucking wrong, too. I have to be available. That's why I'm so successful. I respond immediately. If they need something done, I get it done that fucking second. Yesterday took a toll on my work already. I'm going to have to bust ass to get it back up. And his internet is so god damned slow that everything is taking longer than it should.

"You don't understand, I have to be available," I say.

"You want to be able to go online without being monitored?" he asks.

I nod my head even as I realize how ridiculous my request is. But he said he'd give me my life back. And this is my life. It's my passion.

"Alright, kitten," he says as though it's perfectly normal. As though there's no harm whatsoever in allowing me to do this without him here. I remember the ping from his earlier text. But that had to have been a coincidence.

Hope rises in my chest. Maybe I can get the fuck out of here after all. I don't need him fucking with my emotions and manipulating me into fucking begging him like he just did. He hands me back the computer and I take it as gently as possible to hide my intentions. I'm going to escape. I just need to figure out how.

CHAPTER 16

ANTHONY

I have shit to do, but I'm waiting. I know she's going to push. Especially after leaving her all hot and panting for my touch like I did. I walk about five steps away from her door and lean against the wall. If I've learned anything about my sweet little pet, it's that she acts on impulse. And right now, she's not too happy with me. But she needs to learn that she's not always going to get what she wants. I readjust my erection and think back to how she writhed under me. She fucking wanted me. But she didn't beg. And I had to get the fuck off of her before I broke my word.

I log on to my phone that's now on silent and go through the alerts. There's a logger on her computer and I set up a script to monitor what she's doing. Even shit that she types, but doesn't send. Titles of books or authors that could trigger clues. Words and phrases or certain sites that she'd think of going on. There's also a feed. I can watch everything she's doing as she's doing it. And I can veto it, too. I go through the list of triggers again. Three triggers--*Comfort Food*, "help me, please", and "taken." The last two triggers seem harmless enough in context, but that first one? I know what my kitten was up to. I thought about going over and busting her ass. But I'm gonna wait until she makes a clear offense. Something she can't deny is wrong.

I lean my head against the wall realizing what that means. I don't want her back in the cell. But she's going back. I'd bet my life on it. And that fucking sucks. I was hoping we'd make more progress; I was sure we would, but I was wrong.

Ping. Another notification pops up and I'm quick to hit--blackout. My kitten is about to freak the fuck out. I hear her cuss and move around in the room. Her screen just went black, and she sure as fuck knows why. I pocket my phone and punch in the key code to her room. I check my other pocket for the sash and it's there. Good. I'm gonna need it. I've got all sorts of shit I use for work out here in the hall. She doesn't need to see that and think it's for her.

I open the door and examine her room. She's nowhere in sight, and the room is silent.

I close the door behind me quietly. "Kitten," I call out for her, but she doesn't respond. Even I have to agree the calm manner I'm calling out with is creepy as fuck. But it's better that I'm calm. She's already on edge, and I can't push her away with my anger. She's scared, and I don't need her to turn violent. She would. I'm sure she would.

"Kitten, you will answer me." I take a few steps past the living room area and into her bedroom. "Do you want to make this even harder on yourself?" I ask. There's only a hint of anger in my words. I don't want her scared of me. I want her scared of displeasing me. There's a very big difference.

"I'm sorry, Anthony." I hear her words as I open her closet doors. They came from behind me. I look at the bed, and then at the space underneath. Oh, how...pitiful. I walk over and stand where she should be able to see me, if she has a view from wherever she is under there. At least I feel a little relief knowing she responded to me at all. That's a good sign.

"Kitten, you need to come out," I say.

"Please," she begs with a sob. She sounds remorseful and truly upset. And she should be.

"Please what, kitten?" I ask.

"Please don't kill me," she whimpers. I close my eyes and pinch the bridge of my nose as I exhale with frustration.

"I'm not going to hurt you, kitten." My words come out soft to help her relax somewhat. "I can promise you I won't. You already know your punishment." I hear her sniffle amidst the small sounds of movement. "I knew I'd have to wait to leave. At least I can say I'm only mildly disappointed that you disobeyed me so quickly. It's best we get this out of your system now." A moment passes, and she doesn't appear. I'll give her one more chance.

"Come out now." I make my voice harder and then regret that I did. She cries louder, but I still don't hear her moving to come out.

"If I have to come get you, you're really gonna regret it." The thought of dragging her out makes my cock jump in my pants. Fuck, I would fucking love it. I can't wait until we're at that point. Once that pussy is all mine, I want her to hide from me so I can punish her. I want to punish that ass with my dick, rather than my hand. Soon. I remind myself that I just need to be patient. If I did it now, it would ruin everything.

As I open my eyes, I see her sliding out. Her small body drags on the floor as she squeezes between the floor and the frame. Poor Catherine. She looks so despondent.

I stand with my arms folded across my chest and watch as she slowly stands up. She hangs her head low and she's angling her body in a way that makes it obvious that she expects me to hit her. She should know that I won't. But she's still going to be punished. It will help her. I remind myself that this needs to happen. She'll learn. I only want the pain to be pleasurable. And this punishment will contain zero pleasure.

"I had to try." She looks at the ground as she speaks, and I fucking hate it.

"You didn't. You didn't *have* to." It makes me angry that

she thinks she needed to disobey me. She needs to get over that shit. Hopefully a day and a half in the cell will be enough. "You *chose* to."

I pull out the blindfold and she submits to me, turning around so I can tie it and lead her to the cell.

We're quiet the entire way to the cell. The only sounds are the echoes of our footsteps and her uneven breathing. I pet her back with every step and at times she seems like she's ready to lean into me, but she doesn't. She's rejected my touch, my comfort, my trust. I sigh heavily as I take off the sash and prepare to leave her, but then I see mascara running down her cheeks as she crumples onto the floor and scoots away from me.

I need to wait until she's calm. She'll learn to accept her punishments. When she's fully aware of what she'll receive in return, that knowledge will keep her from failing to obey me.

I lean down and stroke her cheek. "It's alright, kitten." She doesn't respond, but she doesn't move away from me either.

"I'll have to go get your things without you. You need to tell me everything you want." I don't tell her that her things will always be there for her. I plan on keeping up with her mortgage and bills. Every contact that she gets will go through me, and to her, and then back to the sender. I don't need any red flags to go to the WPP. Fuck that.

The reminder of life outside of these walls pisses me off.

None of that will be necessary if I have to kill her at the end of the month. I press my lips into a straight line. That's not going to happen. I've only just started to have my time with her. Vince will give her to me. I bring in so much fucking money with these hits. He'll give me this. I just need to deal with the Cassanos.

"I--" She hesitantly looks at me and then back down, grabbing onto her fingers nervously. "I have a pair of earrings in my armoire." She speaks so quietly I can hardly hear her. "I need them. Please." She looks up at me with a pleading expression. "They're owls," she says as her voice cracks and she breaks down at my feet. She bends over with her hands on the floor as a wretched sob heaves through her chest. She needs me right now. This is more than just being sorry about getting caught. It's more than being ashamed that she broke the rules, or fearing that I'm going to hurt her.

I sit on the floor next to her and pull her shaking shoulders into my embrace.

"I'll make sure to get them. Anything else?" I speak softly into her hair and breathe in her sweet scent. Her small body is so warm against me. She's leaning into me like I'm her savior, regardless of the fact that I'm about to leave her in a cell with nothing.

After a few minutes of me gently petting her back and her hair, she pulls away slightly. She still doesn't look me in the eyes. "I can't remember." She wipes her eyes and sighs. "Nothing I can think of."

I'm going all the way to her house for one pair of earrings.

It's nearly two hours away. Obviously they mean something to her though. I give her a curt nod that she doesn't see, because she's not looking at me.

I take her chin in my hand and force her eyes on me. "You'll be here until tomorrow night. That's your punishment."

She noticeably swallows, but nods her head and manages to push out, "Yes, Anthony." Good girl. She's taken this well at least.

I have to leave her. I don't want to, but I do. "I have to go, kitten," I tell her gently. I hate that I'm leaving her in here, but she knew the consequences. It's important for her training that I stick to my word.

She leans against my leg as I pet her hair. I know she doesn't want me to leave, but I have to.

I pat her head to let her know I'm going, and she responds by looking up at me with sad brown eyes, glossed over with tears.

"I promise I won't do it again," she says, but her plea is weak. She's resigned to her fate.

"You earned your punishment, kitten. I'll be back to give you dinner," I say.

With that I turn and leave her. She barely grips my leg, but releases me without me having to scold her.

It fucking hurts my chest as I press the keys to leave.

I wish she hadn't done that shit.

But if I was her, I would have done it, too.

CHAPTER 17

ANTHONY

Rigs, Vince's giant ass lab, is lying pathetically on the floor begging. He's a good-looking dog. I look to Vince and say, "See, told you the kids would ruin him. He's a biscuit-begging mutt now."

Vince shakes his head and my brother laughs, taking another drink of his beer. All the women are in the living room with the kids. Usually Rigs goes where the kids go, but we're still in the dining room, and so is the food. Smart dog.

"He was so fucking good before the kids. You could drop a steak a foot from his face and he wouldn't move," Vince jokes, and we all have a laugh even though he's shaking his head.

"God, the kids. Cockblocking and dog ruining," Tommy

says with his hands over his eyes. He's worn the fuck out with the little ones. But he still says it with a smile.

"Gotta love 'em though," Vince answers.

"I need another beer," Tommy says with a touch of humor.

"Grab me one, too?" I ask him. He gives me a nod and heads out. Vince gets up from his seat to pour more Jack in his glass.

As soon as no one's looking, I give the dog the last meatball from my plate. He swallows it down so fucking fast there's no way he even tasted it. I chuckle at him and watch him lift his head up higher so he can see what's left up here. Greedy ass dog.

Vince takes the head seat again and leans back with his glass at his lips. When he looks at me this time, there's tension surrounding us. I know what it's about, too. I've been waiting for it.

"We gotta talk, Anthony," he says.

Tommy makes his way back with the beers and passes me one. I don't want him in here for this though. I don't want him to know about Catherine. She's my secret. She's *mine*. I wish even Vince didn't know. It kills me that he does. Even worse is that I know he doesn't understand.

"Hey, bro, could you give us a minute?" I ask Tommy as I pop the cap off my beer. He looks between me and Vince with a touch of confusion, but nods his head with a bit of a frown.

"Everything good?" he asks. He's always worrying about me. He always has.

Vince and I both nod as I answer, "Yeah, I just need a minute."

"Suit yourselves," he says, grabbing a bun off the table. He whistles at Rigs and the dog bounds off after him, wagging his tail.

"You need to take care of her," Vince says the second Tommy's out of earshot.

"See the thing is, I *am* taking care of her, Vince. We had a deal." I put my beer down and lock eyes with him. "I paid, and she's mine."

"They seem to think otherwise." He says the words as though them backing out is acceptable.

"That's their fault. They made an assumption. They were wrong."

"They give us almost thirty percent of the income from the hits, Anthony. *Your* income. You really wanna piss them off?" he asks.

"I couldn't give two fucks about them, to be honest." I say it with a hint of menace in my voice. I take another drink, trying to calm myself down.

Vince looks at me with hesitation. "What's gotten into you? You aren't usually like this."

"Like what? Stubborn? Opinionated?" I ask. I know I'm pushing my boundaries. But I don't care. I'm always on the outside with them. I have been for most of my life. I never ask for anything. This is the first and only request I've ever made.

"Look, I know you have your issues and all." He talks in a hushed tone, and I fucking hate it. I hate how the entire family feels sympathy for me because of that shit with my mother. They talk about it behind my back. I know they do. But they fucking fear me, too. I'd rather have the fear than the sympathy any fucking day.

"My issues?" I ask, putting the beer down on the table and staring back at Vince like he's going to have to spell it out.

I look back at him, and suddenly he's not the Don. He's one of the boys huddled around the broken, bloodied dumb fuck we were supposed to teach a lesson.

They all stare back at me. I can feel their eyes on me as I breathe heavily and try to calm myself. My shaking fists are dripping with his blood. He had it coming to him. They all know I'm fucked up. He should've known better than to push me.

"You alright, Anthony?" *Tommy lays an unsteady hand on my shoulder. I look up at him and past him to see the other guys. They look nervous as fuck. Like they could be next. I'm not a savage. I can contain this. I do contain it. Every fucking day.*

"Good job, Anthony." *Vince says as he looks between the dead fuck and me.* "Pops is gonna be proud." *He says the words, but there's more to it than that. I don't know if it's jealousy, or if he hates that he fears me.*

That day I decided not to give a fuck about any of them. All of them except for Tommy. Tommy's all I have.

That was the day they started giving me a little more space than normal. I had to push my humor onto them to loosen them up. But it wasn't quite the same. Not with us doing jobs together. Thank fuck for Uncle Dante. He gave me the hits and the other shit I could do on my own. It was a release for me, but more than that, it saved me from being the social pariah. I always knew they felt that way about me. But having Vince say the words...fuck, it hurts to know it's true.

"You know what I mean, Anthony." He straightens his back and meets my gaze head on. I have to hand it to him, he deserves to be boss. But I can fucking smell his fear from here.

"I bought her, and now she's mine. That's what happened. End of story," I say flatly.

"It's not the end. You also agreed to one month, and that's what they were told," he says.

"I didn't--" I start to answer, but he cuts me off.

"You did." He says the words with finality. I never should've said it was his call. It pisses me off. I shouldn't have trusted him. It wasn't his decision to make.

"I have work to do, and I need to get home to check on her before bed."

"Check on her?" he grunts a humorless laugh and it takes everything in me not to plant a fist on his jaw. I can hear Aunt Linda in the kitchen and the kids playing not twenty feet from us. I clench my fists at my side, but hold back. I finish the beer and grab my keys off the table.

Checking on her is my job. This isn't about getting laid, it's not about fucking her or using her, or demeaning her. That's not what I want. This is more than that. It's deeper than Vince could possibly know. It's about having someone *need* me. And she does, whether Vince likes it or not.

"I mean it, Anthony," he says to my back.

I don't answer him. I still have time with her. It may be best that I don't get too attached though. I close my eyes as I open the door and step out into the night.

The cold air whips against my skin. She's in a cell for trying to get away from me, for fuck's sake. I shake my head and feel torn. I thought this would be perfect, but it's not.

I'm just damaged goods. That's all I am.

Perfection doesn't exist. Neither do fantasies.

CHAPTER 18

CATHERINE

I wake to the faint hum of the lights being turned on in the cell. I'm so fucking cold. The only thing he gave me besides the chair was my chenille throw. At least it was freshly washed. Not like that matters now though, since I've got it bunched up underneath me as a makeshift mattress. It fucking sucks.

The lock clicks and the doorknob turns. I quickly get into position. I'm mindful of keeping my hands exactly how he likes them.

My heart flutters in my chest. Last night he didn't stay. He left me with dinner and watched me eat it in silence. An air of disappointment and distrust surrounded him. I don't understand why he's angrier with me now than he was when he put me in here. I feel like I'm failing, and I don't know what I'm missing. I wish I could go back in time. If I could, I would.

He walks in front of me and stops. I look up at him, hopeful that today he's in a better mood.

"Good morning, kitten," he says simply.

"Good morning, Anthony," I respond.

He puts a bowl down on the floor. It's oatmeal with strawberries and cream. It's my favorite. I had a shit-ton of it at my house and I find myself wondering if he went back there. I want to know if he was able to find the earrings, but I don't ask. I stay in my position and look at the bowl and then back at him. He didn't feed me dinner last night like he did before, and I didn't think much of it. But this morning reminds me of the first time we met, of him feeding me.

He shakes his head no and walks to the chair to sit down. "You don't get my touch in here, kitten. That's part of your punishment."

My heart sinks as I pick up the bowl and watch him cross his arms. I feel fucking sick. He's so fucking angry with me, and I don't know that I'll ever be able to take it back. I had to try though, didn't I? *No, I chose to.*

"I got your earrings. You won't get them until you're back in your room." His voice has a hard edge.

"Thank you." My voice cracks, and I have to take a deep breath to steady myself.

"What do they mean to you, kitten?" The use of my pet

name brightens my spirit and my chest fills with hope. It's not lost on me that if he decides not to forgive me, he could kill me. He *will* kill me. It's not just that though. I hurt him. I disappointed him. That shouldn't affect me like this, but it does.

I jump at the opportunity to answer. And at the chance to do something and to talk to someone after spending hours alone and barely sleeping in this room. "They were my mother's." I wipe the sleep from my eyes and clear my throat of the knot growing there.

"I'm sorry for your loss." His words are short and simple, but I can hear the faint compassion in his voice.

"Cancer," I answer as I stir the oatmeal. I'm hungry, but it's not nearly as appetizing as it was before. I don't talk much about her. I don't like remembering.

"I know," he says, not moving from his position. A small, sad smile forms on my face. Of course he knows.

"Do you want to play the game, kitten?" he asks.

"Yes," I immediately answer, and I don't even care that I sound desperate. I fucking hate that game, but I want him to stay.

"How does a girl like you wind up with a man like Lorenzo?" I hate his question. I don't want to talk about him or think about him. I have to work hard not to show how upset it makes me.

"I just needed something different. He distracted me, I guess." He did. I nod my head thinking about how I went from crying all day and struggling to pack up my mother's things, to getting drunk and doing things I never thought I would.

"So you went for the *bad boy*." He says the words like he's disgusted by them, which is fucking ironic.

"It works in the books," I barely get the words out. It's what I really wanted. I wanted to find love. Even if he didn't love me back at first, I was hopeful that I'd eventually find my own happily ever after. I thought I'd found a hard man who'd melt for me in time. Instead I found an abusive fuckface. 'Cause let's be real, that's what life gives you when you go out looking for Mr. Wrong.

"Your turn, kitten. One question." He leans forward in his seat like he's ready to leave, and I hate it.

I ask the one thing that's been on my mind for hours. One thought that sickens me. I wish he'd just hit me and make that my punishment. I'd let him beat me if it meant this would be over with.

"I'm surprised you haven't hit me," I say. He makes no move to answer me, and there's no change in the expression on his face. He's silent for a moment.

"I don't want to hit you," he finally answers. And I believe him.

"Why?" I just don't understand. Lorenzo thrived by showing me how strong he was. He fucking loved dominating me physically. I keep expecting the dams to break and for Anthony to let loose on me. I expect to be physically punished for my infractions. I'd thought he was restraining himself before, but now that I look back on it, I don't think he was.

"I'll never hit you. My father used to hit my mother, and it made her do bad things. I don't want that for you or anyone else."

"I'm so sorry." My heart twists with agony. That's a horrible thing to grow up with. I can't even imagine. My own father passed away when I was younger in a car crash. I hardly remember him. I can't imagine growing up in a house with abuse. My eyes search his, but he gives nothing away. "Bad things?" I ask tentatively.

"She beat me instead since she couldn't hit my father back." My mouth falls open with a gasp as he continues. "I was young, but I remember." His voice is flat and devoid of emotion. My heart is fucking destroyed by his words.

"I'm so sorry." I shake my head, as though I can deny the truth.

"She's dead now." My throat closes and dries. His life just gets sadder and sadder. I want to scoot closer to him, but it's obvious he doesn't want that. He doesn't want sympathy. I don't even think he'd accept compassion.

"Did your father...?" I don't finish, but I don't have to. He nods his head once with his eyes locked on mine.

"He killed her when he saw what she's done; snapped her neck in front of me. He thought he was doing the right thing."

My mouth hangs open in shock.

"I don't even know if he ever hit her or if he didn't love her. I know next to nothing about what their relationship was like, apart from what my mother told me. We never talked about it. She beat me and he killed her for it. That's all I know." He gives me a sad smirk. "There's a lot of, 'let's not talk about it' that happens in the familia."

"I'm so sorry." I repeat my words; I don't know what else to say. I feel pathetic that I have nothing to offer him. Tears threaten to fall. I feel nothing but empathy for him and the pain he must've felt. Both our mothers are dead, but mine never hurt me. I never once questioned if mine loved me.

"Don't be. My brother's always been there. And in a lot of ways so has my father." His hard expressions soften somewhat. "I have to go, kitten," he says.

"No, please," I say. The bowl falls from my lap to the ground as I crawl closer to him.

"Are you telling me no? Are you the one giving orders now?" My shoulders hunch in as I lower myself to the ground. Tears slip down my cheeks. Some for me, but most are for him. I want to hold him and soothe the broken part of him I know exists. But I also need to be touched. I can't stay here like this.

"Please, Anthony. I want to earn your touch." I say the words with the desperation I feel.

His eyes widen with surprise and the darkness that's plagued him since last night seems to lift slightly.

"What are you thinking, kitten?" he asks.

"Whatever you want. I'm yours." I've never said truer words.

"Lie on your back and spread your legs for me." He gives his command and I obey. I refuse to think of this as anything but meeting my own needs. I need to feel something other than this emptiness.

"Good kitten," he says and rises from his chair. "I'll come back tonight once your punishment is over."

With that, he leaves me.

Alone and pathetically bared to a man who won't touch me, I curl up on my side and cry. I don't know how long, but it doesn't matter. It's not long enough to fill the emptiness inside of me.

Chapter 19

Catherine

It's been over a week. He's barely touched me or said anything to me. It's as though my punishment still hangs over my head. All I have is this room and my laptop. *My old life.* I'm surprised he gave it back to me.

I feel empty though. It's like I've hurt him. It's like he doesn't want me. I don't understand it. *He* doesn't trust me.

A few nights ago he came for me. Only one night has he touched me like he did before. He said I was being good and I deserved a reward. He laid me across his lap and instead of making my ass red with his hand, he pumped his fingers in and out of my needy pussy. He knows that I've been craving his touch, but I haven't begged him to fuck me yet. I just haven't been able to get the words out.

"I want my mouth on you." I remember him saying that as I came on his hand. I can't deny that I wanted it, too.

He throws me on my back and I part my legs for him. His shoulders dive between my legs, but he bites my thigh. I scream out as his fingers stroke my G-spot. It feels so good. My body heats with need. I wait for his lips to touch my clit. But they don't. He sucks my inner thigh, so tantalizingly close but not quite there, and I wish that touch was where I need it most.

I beg him, "Please, Anthony. Please!" He pulls away from me and fingers me until I cum again from the ruthless pace of his touch.

I'm breathless and limp. I lie there until my body's no longer useless.

I press my fingers against my hot cheeks. Everywhere still feels hot, but my cheeks and chest are burning. Each time he touches me, it's more and more intense. I've never been so...sated in my life. It's more than foreplay. It's like he's taking me higher than I could have taken myself. And what's better is that he wants to push me there.

It's a game to him though. I can't forget. It's not like he's doing a good deed. He wants me to break for him. He wants me to beg. And I did. The memory reheats my body. He said he wanted to put his mouth on me, and I begged him to, but he didn't.

"I said yes." The words tumble from my mouth without a filter. He looks up at me with a neutral expression. "I heard you."

His admission makes me feel self-conscious. Why have me beg for him if he wasn't going to do it? I don't understand why, but it hurts. I pull the duvet up and around my body and scoot up into a seated position. I can see him putting his shirt back on, but I don't really watch him. I just want him to leave.

"You hesitated." Anthony sits on the bed next to me, making it dip. I look up at him through my lashes but I keep my mouth shut. An apology is trying to climb out, but I won't. I'm not going to apologize for not begging quicker. I fight to keep my face from showing my anger. He cups my chin and leans down to kiss me and I lean into him. I can't help that I want his affection. I won't deny that it fills a deep need I'm only now realizing how much I craved. His lips break from mine and I miss them instantly. I know he's leaving, and I'll be alone until tomorrow.

He gives me a soft smile and rubs his nose against mine. It makes me close my eyes. When I open them he's already across the room. Before he leaves he says, "Next time you'll answer more quickly, kitten."

The words come out before I'm even aware I'm saying them. "Yes, Anthony."

That was three days ago. And he hasn't touched me or hinted at anything else since. Most of the time I think he regrets this. I think he really doesn't want me anymore. I'm not the pet he wanted. But then I think maybe I'm just missing something. Maybe he's waiting for me. If that's the case, I'm ready to beg. I hate this empty feeling that I'm not wanted or that I'm not good enough.

I look at the clock and it's almost three. He's come in everyday to check on me around now. My fingers tap on the keys, but I'm not typing anything. I'm just waiting for him. My work's done anyway. It'll pile up quickly, but it can wait.

Finally, I hear the sounds I'm used to. He's coming. I set the laptop to the side and climb to the foot of the bed. I kneel there for him and wait.

I hear the door open and I watch as he walks into my room. He gives me a small smile and it fills my chest with warmth.

"Kitten," he greets me as he walks toward me.

"Anthony," I say his name with a breath of reverence. He cups my chin and I lean into his embrace.

"How are you today?" he asks.

"Well." I look up at him through my lashes and almost don't say the words, but I need to. I need to let him know that I do want this. I'm sick without his presence. "I missed you."

His eyes light with a flash of something I don't recognize. "I missed you as well."

I just need him to touch me and tell me that I've been good. I've done everything he's told me to. I don't understand why he's treating me so differently now. I'm doing everything I can to prove I won't betray his trust again.

"Will you stay with me?" I ask him.

"I have to work tonight, kitten." I love the use of my pet

name. "I only came in to check on you."

"Please, don't leave me here." I grip onto him and he gives me a look of reproach, but I don't let go.

"This is your room." He looks around the gorgeous suite. "I made it just for you."

I don't want this room if it comes with this feeling of nothingness. I need more. I say the words that have been eating me alive.

"I want to prove to you that I'm yours." I feel so needy, so pathetic. I just don't want him to turn me down and throw me away. I don't give a fuck about anything other than being his. I need his touch. I need the taste of the fantasy he gave me before I betrayed him. I've had a lot of time to think, and I want to try. I may be forced to be here, but I want to give in to the temptation. I'm scared to do it, but I have nothing to lose. I can't deny that a growing part of me finds all of this incredibly sexy.

He says nothing and a feeling of complete despair washes over me. "Please." I cling to him, needing something. I can't keep going like this. I'm trying so hard to be his, but I feel like I mean nothing to him. I'll beg him; I'm ready.

He strokes my hair and says, "We'll see when I get back."

"Can I give you something now, please?" I would do anything to hear him tell me I'm a good girl.

"Please, Anthony. I want to please you," I say.

A moment passes as he searches my face for something.

And then my eyes fall to the button on his jeans. I watch as his deft fingers easily undo them.

"On your knees, kitten." His voice holds a hint of danger to it as he issues the command. I love it. It reminds me of our first morning together. Well, technically the second. Before I disobeyed him. Before he changed.

I climb off the bed and move to my knees for him.

He strokes himself once in front of me. I lick my lips and wait patiently. If he wants me to suck him off, I will. I want to. I'll make him want me. I know he will. My pussy clenches and heats with excitement as I watch him stroking himself, his eyes focused on my mouth. This turns him on as much as it does me. The intensity of my desire rises. I have a power over him that he can't deny and it's simply intoxicating. I'll make him need my touch.

"Open, kitten," He starts to put the head of his dick on my tongue, but then he pulls away. "No teeth this time," he says with a dark look in his eyes. I nod my head and feel a wash of shame. I'd never do that. Never.

Maybe the old me would have considered it, but the new me...Mentally I shake my head. I had an old life before my mother passed away, and a new life after I went into witness protection, but deep down I'm the same person I've always been. It's just taken my time here with Anthony to really open my eyes to that fact. My training with him has awakened all my hidden and taboo desires. All the things I always thought could never be more than unrealized fantasies. But we can make our fantasies come true together. I just need to submit to him fully.

I feel a small sense of shame that he feels like he'd have to tell me that. I've changed. I've accepted that I'm his, but he isn't acting like I have. I open wider and wait for him. I want him to know I'm willing. I want him to see me as his so I can really live this dark fantasy.

He fills my mouth with the head of his cock, but then pulls back. "Only the tip kitten. No more than that."

I look up at him and nod with my mouth still open. I'll take anything he's willing to give me.

I moan around the head of his cock and swirl my tongue. His large hand strokes his cock and I wish I could do it for him. My fingers dig into my thighs as I gently rock back and forth doing everything I can to get him off. The tip of my tongue dips into the slit of his dick and I fucking love that he hisses and throws his head back.

I'm so wet for him, so needy. But this is all for him. I want to take him all in. I want to shove him so far down my throat that I choke on him. But I obey him. It takes all of my willpower, but I do it. I suck his head so hard it hollows my cheeks. He takes it out with a pop and smacks it against my cheek.

"Again, just like that," he says with a ragged breath.

I look into his eyes as I do it again and I see the moment he reaches his climax. He keeps my gaze and parts his lips with an admiration I've never seen before. Hot jets of his cum stream into my mouth and I'm quick to swallow it and gently suck him until he's done.

"Swallow it all," he says with a rough groan that makes my pussy clench. I do.

He pets my hair as I wipe the corners of my mouth. I lick his slit until he takes it away from me. I bite my lip, staying exactly in the position he left me in. I'll prove to him that I've learned to listen and that I can obey.

"I'll be back tonight, kitten," he says as he buttons his pants. "Beg for me tonight, and you can have whatever you want."

Chapter 20

Anthony

"Do you know what I don't want to be doing right now, Tommy?" I ask my brother.

"Taking this guy out with me?" my thickheaded brother answers. He used to be the muscle for the *familia.* Now he does hits with me. He just happens to fucking suck at some aspects. Give him a long-distance kill, and he's fine. Up close though, and he's sloppy as fuck.

I tap my pointer to my nose.

We're in a car parked across from Barcode. It's a dive bar on the strip and we've been waiting in the dark for a good two hours now. I keep looking at the monitors in the app on my phone. My kitten's been lying in bed reading and stretching or doing some yoga shit on the floor. I want to get back to her. I want to hear her beg for me. Even more, I want to hear those soft moans from her lips as she cums on my dick.

Instead I'm doing this stupid shit 'cause Tommy didn't want to do it on his own.

"Hey, I don't wanna be out here either. I've got more important shit going on, but we need to take this guy and not just kill him."

I can't blame him for being hesitant to take over and do this without me. I grunt a response and then think about his wife and my sweet little niece as I say, "Yeah you do. You gotta be happy to not be hearing all that screaming for once."

He smiles back at me. I don't fucking get it. He's overjoyed about that little bundle of high-pitched lungs. She is a cutie, but damn, if only they could come out already talking and walking.

"You know she's adorable." He smiles back at me, finally taking his eyes away from the bar across the street.

"She's real cute, Tommy." I can admit that. She's adorable when she's sleeping. "You did good. I'm proud of you."

"I meant what I said, it's gonna happen for you. You don't have to be so fucking jealous all the time," he says.

I hold in a deep laugh. Jealous isn't quite the right word. I made up my mind a long time ago. That world isn't for me. I'm not meant to be a husband or a father. I don't have that ability. I know I'm capable of love, because I truly love my *familia*. But I'm fucked in the head. I know I am. They know I am.

There's no reason for me to ever think about taking that path in life. Even with my sweet Catherine.

My thoughts are interrupted when I notice the movement from across the street. I lean forward in my seat as the fucker on our list exits the bar, nearly stumbling as he lights a cigarette. Tommy starts talking, but I simply nod my head and keep my eyes on the dumb fuck who skimmed off the top of our shipment. He fucking knew better. He's been on the inside for a while now. He's almost a made member. Maybe he got tired of waiting. Maybe he just wanted the money. I don't know, and I don't care. I just need two pieces of information from him and then we can get this shit over with.

Who'd he sell it to, and where's the money?

Louie leans against the wall, taking a few puffs of his cigarette. I'm sure he thinks he got away with it. He looks like he doesn't have a care in the world.

I take a look down the street and it's busy as fuck. There's a narrow alley in between the two shit buildings. I'm sure we could take him for a walk. I've gotten away with that shit before, and I know I could keep his ass from screaming too loud.

"Let's do this shit," I say.

Tommy looks at me anxiously. "Out in the open?" he asks.

"Yeah, quick and easy. Let me show you how it's done," I reply.

I step out into the street and walk quickly, keeping my head turned to the right. The only camera is on the side of the street where we parked. But it's angled so they shouldn't get shit. Better safe than sorry though. I already messaged Tony about it. I'm sure the owners won't have any problems erasing the feed tonight. Not when the orders are coming from the Valettis, and their business has been going steady on the loan we gave them.

That's one good thing about the *familia*. We want this town running like a well-oiled machine. And it does.

"Louie." I let a grin slip into place as he kicks off the wall and walks toward us like we're his pals. Like he didn't steal from us.

"Anthony, Tommy, what's up guys?" His words are slightly slurred and it pisses me off. I find when they're drunk they're more likely to piss themselves. More than that, they scream louder, sooner. Tonight that can't happen. "You here for a drink?" he asks.

"Nah," Tommy says and he starts to say something else, but I cut him off. I want him to watch this time, so he can see how it's done and be able to do this shit himself next time.

"Louie, we gotta talk." I say the words firmly and hold his eyes. The fucker holds his breath and I know he's scared shitless. I need him scared, but more than scared, I want him willing to talk and wanting to make me happy. I want him to think I need him.

I lean forward and lower my voice so it seems like I'm letting him in on intel. "There's someone," I start talking then look to my left as a group of young women dressed in sequined, glittery dresses that ride up their asses pass behind us. The street's not packed, but it's busy enough to want to get out of the open so we can have some privacy. I make it a point to look at the entrance to the alley and nod my head. "Let's go down there for a sec."

He starts to put his cigarette down with a look of dread on his face. But I don't want that. I don't want him thinking anything's wrong.

"No need, I don't mind the smoke," I tell him as I start walking ahead of him. "You first, Tommy." I need my brother to catch on to the fact that you don't intimidate targets in public. Not till you have them where you want them. Tommy walks ahead of me with a nod. My brother's smart, even if he does do dumb shit sometimes. He's good at reading people. My back's to Louie. It's a sign that he's not a threat to me. The two of us walk quickly while Louie stays behind for a moment. I keep walking. I know I don't have to tell him twice.

It only takes a minute for Louie to follow us down the alley. It's a few feet wide and blocked off at the back entrance by a dumpster and a chain-link fence. That's not good for the clean-up crew. They're going to have a hell of a time getting the body out without anyone seeing, but that shit's not for me to worry about. Tommy stops about halfway down the alley and leans against the wall. I put my hands in my pockets and face the entrance, waiting for Louie to catch up. He's walking slow, but he sure as fuck isn't stumbling around anymore.

Having the feeling you're about to get caught by the mafia for stealing from them is a surefire way to sober the fuck up.

"What's going on?" He tries to keep his voice from wavering, but he's shit at it. To be fair though, I've tortured a lot of men. And almost all of them are scared at first, even the ones that didn't have shit to tell because they were genuinely innocent. Poor fucks. But this prick is dripping with sweat and his shifty eyes are looking all around us for some hidden door that will lead him to safety. There's no safety here though. Just me, my knife, and Tommy's gun.

I want Tommy to stay out of this one. There's no need for him to get involved beyond keeping this fucker here.

"Listen, Louie. There are some things I need to know before I kill you." His eyes go wide and he takes a step back. He's closest to the entrance, so he's thinking of running.

Tommy's already got his gun on him and we all hear the click of him cocking it back. Louie's eyes lock on the barrel and he nearly tips back as his legs go weak.

He shakes his head and I know he's getting ready to deny it. His hands are raised in the air. "Hey. I wanna make this easy on us all, Louie," I say as I reach into my pocket for a rag as I slowly walk toward him. He takes a step back and I shake my head. His breathing comes in short breaths as he starts spewing off, "Whatever you heard, it wasn't me. I didn't do it." The desperation is clear in his voice.

I wrap the cloth around my fist a few times. It's thick;

thick enough so he won't be able to bite down on my hand. The thought reminds me of my kitten. My sexy-as-fuck little minx, scraping her teeth down my finger. I close my eyes and will the images away. It only fuels my need to get this shit over with. I walk around him and let him retreat until his back is against the wall. We're still almost halfway down the narrow alley. It'd be hard as fuck to see or hear anything from us, as long as he doesn't scream. I look at my left fist, wrapped tightly with the rag and back at Louie.

"You've got one chance. Who'd you sell it to, and where's the money?" I ask him clearly, but I already know I'm going to have to ask again.

He's shaking his head, thinking he can talk his way out of this.

I'm quick to shove my fist in his mouth. He only gets a partial scream out before the rag mutes his frantic screams. He struggles against me, his hands wrapping around my wrist, trying to rip my fist from his mouth. I push my fist harder into his mouth, stretching his jaw. I need to be careful not to break it though. I need this fucker to talk. He's a pretty decent-sized guy and he's doing a good job of throwing my body off of him, but I pull out my knife and hold it to his throat, my forearm bracing his shoulders against the wall. That makes his entire body still. Tommy comes up to my right and holds the gun to Louie's head. Louie looks between the two of us and starts fucking crying. It's pathetic.

"It's just two questions, Louie, then we get to move on from this. You had a chance. You should've taken it." I gave him a warning, and he chose to ignore it. Now he has to accept the consequences.

I nod at Tommy. "Get his hand."

Tommy grabs Louie's right arm, still holding the gun to his head. Louie's quick to pull his arm away, but I dig my knife into his neck, slicing his skin to make a point of what will happen if he keeps this shit up.

He tries to speak into the rag, but it's too late for that. I'll give him a chance in a minute, once the screaming is over with. Louie's got his fist balled, which is a bad move on his part. It would've only been one finger, but with them all bunched together, I slice into his middle finger and thumb as I cut off his pointer. Tommy struggles to keep the fucker's wrist up as I cut his finger off and the dumb fuck screams into the rag.

I let the finger fall and the blood drip down onto the ground as I wipe my knife off on his jacket and push it up to his throat again. I choose a new spot, one an inch up from the first cut. "Stop your screaming," I growl out as I push my fist deeper into his mouth. He whimpers in response, tears flowing down his cheeks as he cradles his arm in his hands.

I talk while I wait for him to calm down. "We have you on tape taking the product, so there's no backing out of this one. You know it. There's only one way out. You just tell me who you sold it to and where the money is, and it's all over."

He cries out something muffled by my hand, but I keep it there until he's calm.

I hold his eyes and wait.

When I take my hand away, his body sags and he closes his eyes. "The Cullums, they bought it."

"Did they know it was ours?" Tommy asks.

Louie shakes his head no.

"Where's the money, Louie?" I bet the fucker's already spent it, but Tony couldn't find it anywhere in his bank accounts.

"I gave it to my brother." Hearing his confession makes my heart sink. I know his brother has a problem with alcohol. They both do. His brother's also a gambler though. And that's not a good combination. I nod my head and wait for him to look me in the eyes.

"You stole from us to get your brother out of debt?" I ask him and I see a flash of hope in his eyes. Like maybe that'll save him. But it won't. As he raises his head to speak, I stab the knife through his neck until it comes out the other side and quickly push it up toward his face, splitting his throat open. It's a silent kill, efficient and quick.

Once his eyes glaze over and his hands fall to his side, I let him drop to the ground. I shake my head as Tommy dials up the crew to come clean this shit up.

He should've known better. No one fucks with us for a reason.

"Damn, Anthony. I need to practice with a knife." I turn

around to look at my brother. He's looking at me the same way everyone always has. Like he fears me, because I do this shit without thinking twice and without feeling remorse. It's simple. He had it coming. It had to happen. Catherine used to look at me like that too; only sometimes though in the beginning. Not anymore. She would if she knew I did this shit. If she really knew who I was. When people break the rules, they die. That's just what happens. Just like my mother. I've come to terms with it long ago. I don't get why everyone else gets so shaken up over it.

I don't feel any different than I did when we walked back here. A little bit of a high on adrenaline, but I just want to get the fuck out.

Tommy says, "I don't think I could do that shit."

"Sure you could, anyone's capable of it." My words remind me of my kitten. Her patient waiting for me, and telling me all the things I want to hear. I don't think she would ever hurt a fly. That's just not the kind of person she is. But if she wanted to kill me, she could. I still expect it at some point. If I was her, I'd try to kill me. The thought makes my blood run cold. At some point she's probably going to try to kill me.

"You alright?" Tommy asks. "It's alright, Anthony. He had it coming to him."

He had it coming to him. I bet that's what she's going to think when she gets the courage to try. I want to believe in her, but ever since that night with Vince, all I keep thinking is that

I'm fucked up. That I was wrong. That this is destined to fail.

I school my expression and look at Tommy as I say, "Let's get out of here."

It's late, but I need her right now. Even if my little kitten wants to sink her claws into me. Even if it's all lies. Even if it's completely fucked up. I *want* her.

CHAPTER 21

ANTHONY

As soon as I put the keys on the table, I make a beeline for the door. I need to get to her. She could be lying to me; she could be gearing up for a fight. I don't fucking know. But right now I want her, and she's ready to beg for me. I'm giving in. Whether it's my dark needs and *issues* or something else causing this impulsive behavior, I don't give a fuck.

I go straight down to the basement. My steps are loud as fuck. I enter the code and swing open the door just in time to see her falling to her knees and breathing heavily. Her hair's a mess, like she was sleeping when she heard me coming. I look past her at the bed and I know that's exactly what happened.

"You want me, kitten?" I walk to her with hard steps.

"You still want to prove to me that you're mine?" I ask her.

"Yes, Anthony," she responds with a deep need in her eyes. I run my hand down my face, knowing this is stupid as fuck. But I'm going to do it. I'm tired of questioning this shit, and I'm tired of waiting.

I lean down and grab her by her waist, carrying her in my arms.

She snuggles into me and stares at my face as I take her up to my room. I want her there. If she's really mine, she'll be mine everywhere. She doesn't look around; she doesn't try to squirm away. She grips onto my shirt and kisses the dip in my neck.

I lay her gently on the bed, but she's quick to pop up on her knees and wait for me.

"You want my dick, kitten?" I ask her.

"Please. Please, Anthony," she begs me as she pulls the nightgown over her head and lies naked on my bed. She's desperate for something from me. Anything. This is what I wanted, but right now, I fucking hate myself for it.

Her lust-filled eyes look back at me as she whispers, "I want to prove to you I'm yours." Fuck, she sounds so sincere.

I nod my head slightly and kick my pants off. If that's what she wants, then she's going to get it. She's going to earn it.

"Fuck yourself on my dick," I command.

I climb on the bed and stay on my knees stroking my cock. Precum's already leaking out and I use it to lube up the head.

She's quick to get on all fours and look back at me over her shoulder. She's too fucking sexy for her own good. She lowers her breasts to the bed and lays her head to the side, keeping her eyes on my dick as she backs her ass up.

I put a hand on her hip to steady her and let her take me in. My breath comes in short pants but I make sure they're low so she can't hear how much I need this. Her ass looks so fucking good. I give it a loud smack. She jumps, and I slip out of her.

"Uh-uh, kitten. You're going to take it. This is your cock right now. Lean back and take it." Her mouth stays parted as she reaches between her legs for my dick. Her small hand strokes the head and I almost cum right there.

Smack! I hit her ass to keep from cumming as she slips the tip inside of her welcoming heat and moves back, stretching her walls slowly around my dick. I watch my cock slowly disappear. So fucking slowly. It's almost too much to take. I ball my hands tightly into fists and fight the urge to just let go. I want to collapse on top of her and bury my head into her neck. I want to bite down on her and fuck her ruthlessly and let my savage beast out. But I need control. I thrive with control. And this is for her, not for me.

She rocks on her knees to get more of me inside her tight little pussy. Fuck, it feels like heaven. I place my hand on the small of her back, but I don't take control. This is for her own needs, not for my pleasure. There's a difference.

I grip her hips, but she's still in control. She slides easily on and off my dick. Her sweet sounds fill the air. That's when it really hits me, she really has given herself to me. I've broken her down to this. She *wants* this. She wants me. She's doing this to please me. What more could she possibly give me? My heart clenches in my chest, and I can't fucking stand it.

Not now. I can't think about this shit right now.

She moans as she slides back deeper and my dick fills her cunt. I can't help the groan that slips past my lips. She feels so fucking good. She rocks forward and I watch as her cream coats my dick. It's the sexiest fucking sight I've ever seen. I want to push deep into her and pound her pussy so fucking hard her body collapses. But not yet.

She fucks herself on my cock, searching for her release, but she's so far from getting that highest high that I can give her. I tilt my hips and thrust back as she impales herself onto my dick. I'm rewarded with a sweet strangled cry of pleasure. "Yes!" she screams out. The sound of her panting and smacking her wet pussy against me is everything I ever dreamed of.

"Please, Anthony!" she cries out as she fucks herself faster and harder. "Please," she begs me.

"Please what?" I ask her. I just want to hear her tell me how much she needs me.

"Please, Anthony," she begs again.

"You want me to make you cum?" I ask her.

"Yes!" she answers.

"You want to cum all over my cock to please me, is that it?" I smack her ass again and again.

"Yes!" she cries out, and it's the last straw. I give in and lose what little self-control I have left.

"Coat my dick with your cum," I growl into her ear as I push her shoulders down and hammer into her. My other hand moves to her slick clit and I strum it until she screaming into the sheets.

Her pussy latches onto my dick and starts milking it with her release. I pump into her harder and faster, and with each thrust her cunt holds onto me tighter, trying to suck me in deep. I nip her earlobe. I bite, kiss and suck all over her neck. Her pussy pulses around me and her body trembles beneath me. She cries out my name, and it's what takes me over the edge. I cum deep inside her. I groan in the crook of her neck, loving that I gave her more than she could give herself.

I slowly release her and her body falls forward and I slip out of her, our combined cum leaking from her pussy.

She lays on the bed panting and curling on her side as I leave her to get a shirt from the hamper to wipe up with. She hums softly in appreciation as I clean her off. She looks so weak and tired as she slips her nightgown back on. I love the sight of my cum leaking out of her tight little pussy, but I need to clean her up before bed. And she's obviously fucking exhausted.

I watch her as I climb in next to her. I expect her to plead with me to stay. I expect her to ask me for something. But she doesn't. She scoots her body against mine and rests her cheek on my shoulder. She cuddles with me. She holds me.

I feel my guard lower from her comforting touch. I should put her back in her room, but I need this as much as she does. I don't think I've ever felt someone hold me with such need and adoration. She rubs her body against mine and I relax into the mattress.

I kiss her hair and pet her back as she nestles into my chest.

"Sleep, kitten," I whisper into her ear.

She looks up at me through her lashes with a small smile. "Good night, Anthony." And she plants a kiss on my lips. I can still feel it as she lies back down and gets comfortable in my arms.

I watch her for hours before I can finally sleep. It never once occurs to me that in the morning she won't be there.

Because I know she will.

CHAPTER 22

ANTHONY

My eyes slowly open and I move to turn onto my side, but a warm and comforting weight rests against my side. *Kitten.* A slow, lazy smile graces my lips. It feels good to wake up next to someone. I never have before. I'm not angry that I let her sleep here last night. But it's a one-time thing.

I stare at her while she sleeps. Her chest rises and falls in a steady rhythm. Her chestnut hair is fanned out on the pillow. I gently brush the hair off her face and fucking love how at peace she is. *With me.*

This is going better than I ever imagined it would. My hand gently eases on her hip as my eyes roam over the dip in her waist. She begged me to fuck her. She wants me. She truly wants me.

I lie back down on my back and sigh. She's seen my darkness, and she craves my touch.

Only because she has no choice. Only because I've conditioned her.

All traces of her warmth and tenderness leave me. And then she stirs beside me. I close my eyes and wait to see what she's going to do. I've no idea what kind of trouble my kitten will get into if I let her roam the house without supervision.

But I'm curious. The idea that locks aren't needed makes me feel powerful, as though I've perfected the relationship I desired. But there's only one way to find out if it's possible.

I feel her body press against mine as her cheek nudges gently against my chest.

She's trying to wake me, but I don't move.

It's been a long time since I've pretended to be sleeping, but I'm still good at it.

Maybe she has no intention of leaving my side. Maybe she's scared of being punished if she does.

I've never said I would. There are no rules against it. But she's made up in her head what this is supposed to be like. She's decided on her own that it would upset me if she wandered around the house without me. That's smart of her, but I want her to push. I want her to learn I can give her freedom if only she'd ask for it.

I wait as she rests on her side and lies still next to me. I know she doesn't want to disappoint me. That's a good thing, but it's also holding us back.

She runs her fingers along my jaw gently, and I have to stifle a soft groan of tenderness so she won't realize I'm awake. I crave her touch as much as she craves mine. But she'll never know that. I can never show her that weakness.

After a moment, she slowly and easily slips off the bed. My little kitten's curiosity got the best of her. Good.

Excitement races through my blood as I hear her walk through the room. I peek through my lashes as she opens the closet.

She can see all the monitors, but she seems unaffected. She knows I watch her. She closes them after a moment of watching the screens flash to different angles in her rooms. She walks slowly and quietly across the room. Her fingers trace over the notebook on my dresser. She slowly opens it and I don't like that.

It's my list. There are names in there she shouldn't know. Her brows raise and she quickly shuts it, taking a step back as though it bit her.

Good girl. She turns on her heel and walks quietly to the door, looking back at me once.

As soon as she's out the door, it's my cue to get up and follow my sweet submissive who's being a bit naughty.

For all I know she could be trying to leave. But I doubt she would. I'm fairly certain she just wants to snoop. I can't blame her. I listen from my bedroom and hear her walk to the next room. The door opens, and she gasps and quickly shuts it.

It's the armory. If she wanted, she could grab a gun in there. But none are loaded and the ammunition is locked away separately, so I'm not worried. But she doesn't. I hear her feet patter faster away from the room and move on to the next door. It's just a guest room, so there's nothing in there, but I can't hear her any longer and I imagine she walked in.

So I decide it's time to put my kitten to the test. My dick hardens at the thought of chasing her. YES! I need this. I want to prepare her first and give her a fair chance to run. I'll catch her though. I'll always catch her; she can never escape me.

I walk silently to the door and peek in. She's fiddling with a wooden puzzle on the desk.

I walk up behind her and quickly press my back to her front, wrap my arm around her waist and cover her mouth with my hand. She screams out of fear but I gently kiss the crook of her neck and she instantly relaxes.

"My kitten is being naughty," I say as I move my hand from her mouth to her throat and the other lifts her nightgown up for me to splay my hand on her bare lower belly. My fingers tease along her clit.

"Did you find anything you shouldn't have?" I ask.

She nods her head obediently. I smile behind her back.

I could ask her what she found, but I already know and I know she'd tell me the truth.

"Did you find anything interesting?" I ask her instead. She

presses her body against mine and her ass rubs against my dick.

"Yes," she says. My dick is so fucking hard for her.

She turns her head slightly to see me and I reward her with a rough kiss.

"I have to punish you, kitten. You should know better than to run off without me," I say sternly.

That knocks the confidence out of her, but she nods her head and stays still in my arms. Once she realizes what this is, she'll fucking love it. So sweet and obedient. She's so fucking perfect.

"This is as much for you as it is for me." She closes her eyes and tries to hide her smile. "It would make me very happy though, if you fought me back." She arches her back and moans softly as I whisper the words into her ear. My fingers slip past her clit and I cup her pussy. She's so fucking wet. "Do you want to fight me, kitten?" I ask.

"Yes," she whispers into the hot air between us as I push my palm against her clit.

"You have five seconds," I say as I pull away and take a step back. She turns to face me, breathing heavily with lust-filled eyes. "Run, kitten," I say.

At my words, she takes off.

It's the longest five seconds of my life. One. She runs out the door, slamming it into the wall. Two. I walk slowly to the hall behind her. Three. Her small feet bounce off each step as quickly as possible. Four. She holds onto the railing and swings around making her way toward the kitchen. Five.

My long strides and taking the stairs three at a time has me on the first floor before she's through the dining room. She doesn't turn around to look at me. Instead she keeps running, pumping her arms and nearly crashing into the table.

She makes a sharp right to go through the hall and I'm on her tail before she can do a damn thing. Her hand grips the doorknob, but she doesn't have time to open it. I grab her waist and pin her to the ground. Her legs thrash against my body and I lay my weight on top of her. She tries to push me off, but I'm bigger. I'm stronger. She doesn't stand a chance against me. My kitten's fighting me though. I fucking love it. Her hands smack against my face and push against my chest.

I growl as I take both her wrists in my hands and pin them above her head, moving them to together so I'm able to hold them with one hand. She continues to struggle against me as I rip her nightgown open with my free hand and pin her down with my hips. I stare down and marvel at her gorgeous body laid out under me. I take one perky breast in my hand and squeeze. Her tiny pink nipples harden and I take it as an invitation to suck them in my mouth one at a time and nibble them as she writhes under me. I pull back and let one out with a pop, leaving a red mark. Fucking beautiful.

Her eyes are shooting daggers at me as she plays along, but they're filled with lust. Her breathing is heavy and labored. I can feel her passion, and that's everything I want. I push my forearm against her chin, pushing her head back so I can lean down and kiss her, knowing she won't be able to bite me.

Her lips are hard at first, but they mold to mine. I'm quick to pull back and keep this fantasy alive.

Her back arches as she tries to buck me off. But I have her right where I want her. My free hand pries between her legs and I push my fingers into her heat. She's so fucking wet.

"You're so fucking dirty. You want this," I say.

I lean down and take her earlobe in my teeth before nipping at her skin, leaving tiny pink marks all over her neck.

"Please!" she cries out.

"Your cunt is *begging* me to fuck you," I whisper in her ear.

"Is that what you wanted, kitten? You wanted me to punish you like this?" I ask as I push a third finger in and pump them in and out as she begs me. "Please, Anthony. Please fuck me. Punish me, please."

She stops struggling and moans as I curve my fingers and stroke against her G-spot. My dick is so fucking hard for her.

My blood heats as I line my dick up. Yes! I've waited so long to sink deep into her hot cunt and take her like this.

I don't ease in slowly, and I'm not gentle as I thrust all the way in and keep myself buried deep inside her. Her walls tighten around me as I rip through her, taking her exactly how I've wanted since I first laid eyes on her.

"Fuck!" She screams and cums as her walls stretch and spasm around my cock. Her arousal leaks out between us and onto my thighs. I easily move in and out of her tight pussy, pumping my hips against hers and watching my cock slide in and out.

"Anthony." She moans my name as her body trembles. I pull almost all the way out and then piston my hips over and over, pounding her hips into the floor. Her arms pull against me, but her wrists are still pinned.

I groan as I rut between her legs, watching her tits bounce slightly with each hard thrust of my hips. I push all the way in and grind my pelvis against her clit until her mouth is open with a silent scream and her pussy pops around my dick.

I want her cumming harder than she ever has before, so I don't let up. I grind harder and let her scream and struggle against me with more force than before. Her legs stick out straight and her head falls back hard against the floor as wave after wave of pleasure and heat consume her body. Her eyes glaze over and it's only then that I pull back.

I let go of her wrists so I can spread her legs wider and sink in deeper. My hands grip her thighs as I pound into her.

"Anthony," she moans softly. Her hands travel down her body and then to mine. She moans into the air and her soft eyes stare at me. I reward her by keeping up my relentless pace and pushing the pad of my thumb against her clit.

"Good girl, watch me fuck your pretty little pussy." Her mouth opens as her body stiffens again. Her back bows and she cums a third time. Her nails dig into my back and she urges me to get closer to her body.

I won't deny her. I lay my forearm above her head and let my lips fall onto hers.

She pulls back to breathe and whisper my name. "Anthony, Anthony."

Her fingers grip my hair, holding my lips close to hers.

Over and over she says my name against my lips and then presses them to mine in a sweet kiss.

I cum violently inside her, harder than I ever have before as her lips part and she kisses me with more passion than I've ever felt.

I stay buried inside her, lying down beside her while we both catch our breath.

It's almost been a month; less than two weeks left. I can't let them take her. She's everything I've ever wanted.

I won't let them take her from me. I pull her body closer to me and kiss her shoulder. I won't let her go. They'll have to kill me first.

CHAPTER 23

CATHERINE

I'm still sore from yesterday and last night. Plus this morning. Ever since he had me in the hall, he fucks me nonstop. That's the only difference now. Every morning's still the same otherwise. I get ready and wait for him. I greet him on my knees. And I still stay in my room.

"Your pussy's open for business now." His dirty words echo in my head.

Maybe it's wrong to be so turned on by him, but I don't care. I am. Just thinking about him has my nipples hardening and my back arching off the chair. I clench my sore pussy and instantly hate that he's not here to sate me. I *need* him.

My computer pings and it's only then that I realize my

hand has slipped into my blouse and I'm pinching my nipple between my fingers.

I'm ready for him.

I look down at the message and smile.

My kitten is needy today.

I don't know which camera he's watching so I wave to the screen and nod my head. A blush travels up my chest and into my cheeks.

Get back to work, kitten. I'll take care of you tonight.

I no longer feel trapped. It's like he's given me my life, but filled a hole I was only vaguely aware was empty. All my needs are met. He's seen to that. I have my work, my friends, and a sex life that somehow manages to be hotter than anything I've ever read about. And it's all thanks to him. It hurts to think I may have lived my life without this. Without *him*.

I'm busy editing this piece for my column, and so immersed in getting this paragraph flowing better that I don't hear the lock or the doorknob turn. I don't even hear the door open.

The only thing I can hear is the language of the text over and over that I keep reading in my head. The wording is just clunky and passive, but I don't know how to reorder them. I bite down on my lip and copy and paste a few times, reordering the sentences. My fingers click against the keys.

"Kitten." His voice holds a threat and my body stills. My heart slows but even with the fear of displeasing him clouding my emotions, my pussy aches with need.

I push the chair away and fall onto my knees. I crawl around, keeping my body lowered. Once I see his shoes I stop and sit back on my heels with my hands where they should be. I don't look up though. My heart beats chaotically. I've never not been ready for him. Not since that first day. Every time I hear the click of the lock, I immediately kneel and wait for him. It's been what, maybe weeks at this point? I've been his good kitten and he's kept his word. But this time, I failed.

"I didn't hear you enter." My neck strains as I resist the urge to look at the clock. He usually comes to me around the same time every day. But I got lost in work today.

His hand comes down and rests in my hair. I close my eyes and wait for his response. "Please forgive me, Anthony." The words slip out and I don't try to catch them. My heart swells with agony in my chest. I don't want him upset with me.

"What were you doing, kitten?" he asks as he pets my hair. I open my eyes and finally look up at him. His stubble is a little longer than usual and his hair is as well. It has a tousled look that's fucking sexy.

"Work," I reply easily, and then realize he may want more. "My column is due tonight, but the editor is overbooked. So I'm trying to get it done myself."

He hums, "I see." He looks past me and to the laptop sitting on the desk. I love this little office he made for me. It's so cute with all the book nerd touches, and the large window gives me more sunlight than I'd ever get in the bedroom.

"I think maybe a short break would be nice. We could go get you more flowers." I look up at him with surprise.

"Would you like that, kitten?" he asks.

"Yes, Anthony." I nearly crawl up his body with the need to press my lips to his. But I'm an obedient pet. I keep my hands planted firmly on my thighs and wait for his direction.

"Do you think you're ready to go out?" he asks.

I nod my head. I'm never been outside of these locked rooms. The only exception was that one night. The night I gave myself to him completely. I crave a different environment. A voice deep inside me tells me I can run; I just need one chance. But it's such a small voice, I barely hear it.

"Come, kitten. I think you need a break." My brow furrows with confusion at first and then I realize he meant I need a break from work. He holds his hand out for me and I take it instantly.

He chuckles as he reads the writing on my tank top. It's a racerback that hangs just past my ass and is almost as long as my yellow shorts. The top reads, *Book lovers never go to bed alone.*

I give him a small smile and walk with him as he presses the keys to unlock the door. I know not to look even though he doesn't try to hide the code from me.

It's cold and dark and empty down here. Only a florescent light is above us. It looks so dungeonlike compared to my room. I stay behind him as we walk up the stairs and he presses in keys to another lock. He doesn't give me the chance to look, but I don't mind. I just make a note of it. I'm not sure why though.

My eyes wince as he opens the door and leads me into an open-concept first floor. I take a look around in wonder as if seeing Anthony for the first time in a new light. I don't remember this room when I was out before.

There's a large slate fireplace with a flat-screen television above it. Everything is modern with dark accents and clean lines. It's orderly and nearly barren of any character at all. For some reason it makes me sad. His bedroom was like this, too.

"There's a farm stand down the street," he says as he leads me through the hall without giving me a moment to look around. There are stairs to the right, next to the front door and a hallway that looks like a dead end. *That's where he took me.* A smile spreads on my face as I remember.

He opens the door and keeps my hand in his. I'm surprised to see that his home isn't in the middle of nowhere. It's just a normal house, in a homey cul-de-sac. There are two kids riding bikes to our right, and a third playing with chalk on the sidewalk. Anthony walks to the left and leads me past the houses to a busier street. The sounds of kids playing and a car passing me by seem odd, but comforting. Out in the cabin, I never had this. I like it. It's different.

It doesn't fit with how I pictured Anthony would live though.

"You look surprised, kitten," he says without looking at me. He knew I'd be surprised. He does this often. He says things or asks questions when he already knows what my response will be. He thinks I haven't caught on, but I have. He needs it though. And I'm happy to give it to him.

"I am," I answer honestly.

"Monsters don't live in the dark; they hide in plain sight." His response makes my heart twist in my hollow chest.

"You're not a monster." I spit out the words and look away. I can feel his eyes on me as we stand at the stop sign and a car drives through the intersection. He tugs my hand and we walk to the front of the development and to the right. I can see the stand ahead. It's a shabby-looking shack that's probably been there before the development was built.

"I don't understand." I can't help that the words fly out of my mouth.

"What's that?" Cars fly by us but the breeze still feels fresh against my skin.

"Why do you think you're a monster?" I ask him. Ever since he told me about his mother, I've thought he was broken, but never a monster. He's just missing a piece of his heart. I ache to fill that hole for him.

"Many people have died because of me, kitten. That makes me a monster in a normal person's eyes." I know he's including his mother in that statement. And I hate that.

I stay quiet as we walk closer to the empty stand. There's an old man sitting behind a wooden counter in the shack. Baskets of produce are on the ground, but the flowers are on the counter.

"What are you thinking?" he asks as he lifts a bouquet of purple and pink flowers to my nose. I inhale deeply and close my eyes.

I shake my head at his question and take the flowers from him with a smile. I whisper close to him so the old man doesn't hear, "I don't think you're a monster." My fingers play with the tiny soft petals, but I'm careful not to break them.

He looks down at me while he digs in his pocket for his wallet. "You did at one point, kitten; you were right about me then."

CHAPTER 24

ANTHONY

I'm so fucking tired. I haven't slept in I don't know how many hours. I drag my hand over my face. Fuck, that hit was brutal. It was a former Cassano who double-crossed Marcus. The Don, Marcus Cassano, wanted him to suffer, but I wasn't prepared for that shit. It was a struggle to get him to say a damn word and when he did, it left me frozen with panic.

"Cassanos are coming for you." His dark eyes stare back at me as blood drips from his mouth. The bruises are already starting to show as he wobbles in the chair he's chained down to. Even with all the pain we've inflicted, he laughs at me as I stare back with anger.

He looked right at me and I knew why. Tommy smashed

his fist into the dumb fucker's face. Too hard and too fast though. That's the only info we got from him.

Tommy kept asking me what I thought he meant. I couldn't even look him in the eyes as I lied to him, and told him I had no idea. They want her back. They want her dead. My time's up.

I push the door open to the house and then kick it shut. That didn't go as planned. My eyes fly to the backroom, to where the stairs are to the basement. If I'd die, she'd be in there alone for three days until the door would unlock and let her out. I need to change that shit. She wouldn't be okay for that long. She'd be hurting and hungry. I decide on twenty-four hours, tops. And then all her doors are opening.

I head to my bedroom and go right to the monitors so I can change that shit now. It's done within two minutes and I find myself staring at her sleeping form on the bed. She's got a book in her hands still. I squint at the screen, but I don't recognize which one it is. That stack of books on her nightstand has been there for a week. I don't remember what books I got her though. It's rare that she's got a paperback. She's usually on her Kindle whenever I check on her. I'm glad she found something that I picked out for her. Well, she fell asleep, so maybe she didn't like it all that much. A lazy smile kicks my lips up.

She should be waking up soon and getting ready for me. Waiting for me. I don't give a fuck that I'm worn out. I'm not making her wait. Not today. Not ever again if I can help it.

I need to program something for her to let her know what the hell happened if those doors ever open because I never made it home. Or maybe leave a note each time I go. I don't know what she'd do. Or what she'd think. I drag my hand down my face. I can't deal with this shit right now. I'm tired as all hell.

I drag my ass to the shower. I want to make this fast. I have one thing on my mind, and I need it as soon as fucking possible

All I care about right now is feeling Catherine cum on my dick. It's all I want. I need to feel her body against mine and hear those sweet moans as I push her closer and closer to her release.

I'm in and out of the shower and punching in the code before I know it. She's sound asleep. Doesn't wake up at all. She doesn't hurry to get on her knees and in position like she's supposed to. I walk over to the desk in her room and see on the clock that it's already past 9 a.m. The alarm's supposed to go off at 8 a.m., if she set it. Which she didn't.

She finally had the courage to ask me to change the wake up time from 7 to 8. It's one of the first things she asked me to change. And I was more than happy to do it. I think if she never set an alarm though, my kitten would sleep in all morning. She used to on the weekends when I watched her. But then she'd feel like shit when she woke up to all the work that piled up. I love how she told me that. I love how she's starting to open up to me and really be her true self. It's perfect. *She's* perfect.

I sigh heavily with my eyes closed. I don't fucking want to punish her. I don't want to do this shit right now.

I study her beautiful body on the bed. She's still in her shirtdress from last night. I wonder if she ever even got out of bed after I left her. I bet I just wore her out and she wanted to relax.

I make my way over to the bed and see a pad of paper on the other side of her that was hidden from the cameras. I take a quick look at her scribbles before tossing it onto the nightstand. It looks like my kitten is keeping a diary. I make a mental note to read that later.

"Kitten," I say loud enough that should wake, but not so loud that it should startle her. She rolls her head a bit, but she doesn't wake up like I want her to.

I kick off my pajama pants and crawl into bed with her. I fucking need her right now. I lay my body next to hers and pull her in close, loving her warmth and how she molds her body to mine in her sleep. I gently kiss her neck, hoping that will rouse her. I get a small satisfied moan and a rock of her hips, but nothing else.

"Catherine." My lips barely touch the shell of her ear as I speak just above a murmur. "Wake up for me, kitten."

Her eyes slowly open and seem to settle on my face. A faint smile crosses her face before her eyes shut and she settles her head into the crook of my arm. It makes my heart swell. It only takes a minute for her brain to catch up and her eyes pop open and her body stiffens slightly.

I instantly take her lips with mine, wanting to ease her worry. Her lips are hard at first, caught by surprise, but soon they mold to mine and she leans into my touch. Her small hands press against my chest as my tongue slips into her hot mouth. My hands travel along her body. The feel of the fabric pisses me off. I need to feel her. I grip her dress in both hands, pushing her onto her back and ripping the dress open.

She gasps and clenches her thighs as the buttons pop off and her gorgeous skin is exposed to me. Nothing separates us and that's just how I want it.

I kiss the underside of her breast, taking the other in my hand to feel her soft, supple skin. My tongue swirls along her nipple, leaving a wet trail in my path and then I blow lightly until it's a hardened peak. I do the same to the other side and then pinch and pull them slightly. Her back bows and she moans in complete rapture. The sight of her and the sounds of her pleasure make my raging erection leak.

My fingers dip into her heat and thank fuck, she's already soaking wet. I could play for hours, but not right now. I need to be inside her.

"Spread your legs for me, kitten." She immediately obeys and I don't waste a second as I thrust into her all the way to the hilt. Her eyes open wide and her mouth parts with a silent scream as I pound into her tight cunt.

My fingers dig into her hips as I keep up my ruthless pace.

She screams out her pleasure and claws at the sheets before fisting them and biting down on her lip. I usually start up nice and slow, but I need her. I need this. It's so fucking sexy to watch her take this punishing fuck I'm giving her. Her breasts bounce with each thrust and her lips slowly part in ecstasy as she gets closer to her release. I don't let up. I need more of those noises coming from her lips. I need her eyes to squeeze shut with the intensity of her pleasure.

I'm hitting her cervix every time, but I still don't feel deep enough. I want more. I turn her onto her hip and straddle her leg, bringing the other up to rest on my shoulder. I fuck her hot pussy and there's nothing stopping me from pounding into her farther and deeper than I ever have before. She thrashes on the bed and tries to move away, but I push down on her hip, forcing her into the mattress and making her take every brutal thrust. Her pussy spasms around me and I lose it. I stay deep inside her until her pussy's filled.

It was a quick fuck, but I needed to feel her. I needed to be deep inside her.

She falls to the bed limp, breathing heavily with her eyes closed. Her body rolls slowly onto her side and those sweet lips part as she winces and brings her knees up. For a second I'm worried I hurt her, but then she gives me a sated look with a soft smile.

I still have to ask. I push the hair out of her face and cup her jaw. "You alright, kitten?"

She nods her head slightly in my hand, "Yes, Anthony." She responds like she should, but then adds, "I am." A blush makes her flushed cheeks even redder. "Better than alright."

"I was worried I hurt you." I want to make sure I didn't. I search her eyes for the truth to make sure she's not just giving me the answer that she thinks I want to hear. And they shine back with sincerity.

"I like it when you fuck me like that," she says with a shy smile. I always knew it turned her on, but hearing it makes it different.

I'm fucking exhausted, but I can't sleep here. I need my own bed. I want her companionship though. I don't want to go to sleep alone.

I wrap my arms around her and carry her to my room. Cum drips onto my hip and leg, but I don't care. I kiss her hair as she snuggles into me. I'm so fucking grateful I have her. I don't know what I'd do without her.

CHAPTER 25

ANTHONY

Catherine pulls away from me slightly as we make our way up the walkway. "Are you sure?" she asks. No. I'm not sure. I'm taking her to dinner at my aunt's house, but Vince has no clue. He just needs to see her. He needs to know what she means to me so he can understand. I know she'll be good for me.

"No one has any idea about how we got together, and what we do behind closed doors. That's our business. Just be yourself, and everything will be fine," I tell her with so much confidence in my voice that even I start to believe it. I take a deep breath and open the door. If they've accepted me, they should sure as fuck accept her.

When I open the door, I can hardly fucking breathe.

I've never done this before. I've never asked for acceptance. Maybe because I never wanted it. Maybe because I never thought I could have it. But now I need it.

The guys look over at me and do a double take. Tommy looks shocked at first, and it guts me. He's quick to replace the shock with a wide smile. He's the first to get up and greet us as we make our way to the dining room.

"You brought a friend?" he asks with his eyebrows raised. I look past him at Vince and answer as Tommy pats my back. "Yeah," I say as I bring her close to me. "Meet my girl, Catherine."

My sweet kitten blushes a beautiful shade of red and holds her hand out for Tommy. He chuckles but accepts it, which is a good thing. He doesn't need to have his paws all over her.

I expect a lot of things when I walk in, but I don't expect the cheers from the women and Aunt Linda rushing over to greet Catherine.

It's obvious that she didn't expect that either. She holds onto my hand for dear fucking life. The sounds of the kids playing and the men laughing fills the room. But all I can see is Vince, staring at me like I've betrayed him. And maybe I have, but I had to do this. He needs to know she's not going anywhere.

Vince just needs to understand. What happened wasn't her fault. That fucking prick hit her. She had to leave. He can't expect that she wouldn't have done otherwise. She's strong for what she did.

I'm not going to let him take her. He'll listen and he'll understand. My confidence sways, but I ignore it. *She's mine.*

I stand from my chair in the dining room. Vince is alone in the kitchen. The women are in the den and the men are all in here. Now's my chance to talk to him. I push the chair back, pick up my dishes, and go to him. I need him to hear me out. The tension's been thick between us all night. I just need him to understand. Now that he's seen her, he has to know what she means to me.

"I don't want a rat here. Around my *familia*. In my *home*." He speaks to me in a hushed tone as I set my glass in the sink. It takes all my strength not to break it, not to smash him over the head with it.

"She didn't have a choice, Vince." He just needs to listen to me.

"You're defending her?" I hate that he questions me at all. Someone has to defend her. She's not a rat. She doesn't deserve to be killed, and I won't do it.

"He beat her. When she saw that shit, he made her life hell. She had no choice!"

"He kept her? Are you fucking serious? What'd he keep her as, Anthony? A fucking pet?" He sneers the last word and it's the last fucking straw.

"How fucking dare you!" That fucking prick! He has no right!

"How can you do that to her when you were supposed to kill your own wife? Catherine's not good enough to spare?" I ask, raising my voice.

"I love Elle. She's my *wife!*" he screams at me. I don't hold back any longer, I can't. I let loose and swing as hard as I can, landing a punch on Vince's jaw. He staggers back a few feet, cupping his chin and looking up at me with daggers, but he doesn't make a move to counter. He stands there waiting as he rubs his jaw. He gave me a pass this time. But I won't get another.

He takes two steps and spits in the sink. "If you can tell me right now that you love her, I'll back off. You going to marry her, Anthony?" He's asking like it's a dare. Like he knows me. It fucking tears me up inside that he's right. He doesn't know her. He doesn't know *us*.

"She's as close to a wife as I'll ever have." I didn't even know how true the words were until I spoke them.

"Until you kill her." Vince says the words just as Catherine walks into the doorway. Her mouth parts and her eyes widen as she looks between us.

"Fuck you," I say with disdain at Vince and quickly go to her. I take Catherine by the hand and brush past my brother as he walks into the doorway.

"Whoa," he says with shock. "You guys alright?"

"We're leaving," I answer with my back to him and drag

her out of the house with everyone staring at us.

As the door slams shut behind us, I look at my girl, but I know she's not okay.

My heart hammers with a fear I've never felt before. Although I'm gripping onto her like my life depends on it, she's already gone. I've lost her.

CHAPTER 26

CATHERINE

I sure as fuck wasn't expecting this to be so...comfortable and normal. I'm usually a bit awkward with people—and I still am today, don't get me wrong—but I don't feel the nervous energy I thought I would. I'm able to relax somewhat and just be my usual awkward self. At least around the women.

"So, do you want to be a writer?" Elle asks me. She's Vince's wife. Her voice is soft like you'd think it would be after taking one look at her since she's sweet and petite. Vince isn't. He looks scary as fuck. All the men are intimidating. I'm super fucking happy to be in a room with just the girls.

Being around the men is different. I felt like a sheep brought to the slaughter. I couldn't stop trying to determine which position in the mafia each man had. I couldn't even breathe for the first few minutes. So many fucking flashbacks made me feel like I was drowning. But this is nothing like what I experienced with the Cassanos.

Lorenzo would start talking about things with the other members of his *familia* anywhere, and then look at me like I shouldn't have been there. Like it was my fault. It happened a few times, and then they started doing it on purpose and blocking me from leaving. They liked scaring me and taunting me by calling me the meek mouse. I never felt safe, and they said that was a good thing. Lorenzo said it was good to be afraid. And I was. They made damn sure to keep me afraid.

I stayed with Lorenzo far too long because of that fear and then...well, by the time I had the courage to leave, that's when I actually saw shit. Shit that changed my life forever. I shake my head and try to forget. I don't want to go there in that headspace. Not now.

It's not like that here though with the Valettis. Everything is lighthearted. It took me a while to even want to eat, but when I did it seemed to help. I just kept something at my mouth the entire night hoping no one would talk to me. It's odd how I still felt included in conversations even though I only really ever smiled and nodded. It felt nice though. It's been a long time since I've even talked to anyone. I've been too afraid. Back when I was in hiding, I had the ridiculous idea that the very first person I talked to would somehow know the Cassanos and they would tell them where I was.

But that doesn't matter anymore. I have Anthony now. I've never felt more safe in my entire life than I do tonight. It's the first time I've felt like I could fit in, like I could have a family again. And I want it. I haven't wanted for anything in so long. But I want this.

The kids are all in bed now and the men are in the dining room. Anthony left me alone with the wives. I start to answer Elle's question, but hear a crash of toys from the living room. His aunt, Linda I think, is straightening everything up. I feel weird sitting here not helping. Even though it's not my mess.

"Should we--" I start to ask.

"No," Becca answers before I can finish. She's a bit older than me and she's a no-nonsense kind of person. "Trust me," she places a hand on my forearm, "she will not let you help."

"Okay." I draw out the word and the girls all laugh. It forces a smile from me. I can't help it. I feel included. It's been a long time since I've felt that. My mom was everyone to me. She was my best friend. When she died, I had no one else. It feels good to feel like I belong here. Even though I don't.

"So do you want to write? Or do you just do the columns and blog thing?" Elle asks again and I know she's geniunely interested. She's been asking me questions ever since Anthony told them that I work in romance literature. I literally laughed when he said it like that. *Romance literature*. I love *smut*. That's my genre. Smutty smut smut. I shut the fuck up real quick when he gave me that look though. I'm still a little worried about that look. It could be a good thing though.

"I think I'd like to," I start to answer, but I hear Anthony yell something. We all look to the doorway to the kitchen. But none of the women stand up. Elle grabs my wrist as I start to walk toward him, but I shake her off.

"Don't," I hear her whisper, but I ignore her. The women stand up, but they don't stop me. I know they're right and I should stay away. But something deep down is telling me Anthony needs me. I need to be there for him.

I walk into the kitchen in a daze and see Vince and Anthony yelling at each other. Their hair is a mess and they're both breathing hard. Vince has the start of a bruise showing on his face. Anthony doesn't see me as he says, "She's as close to a wife as I'll ever have." It soothes my soul to hear those words coming from him. But then my heart shatters as I realize what's happening.

"Until you kill her." Vince's words ring out clearly, and I hear them repeated in my head. Over and over. *Kill her.* Anthony finally sees me and I expect to see something in his eyes that proves to me that Vince didn't mean that. That there's no truth there. But it is true. I can barely breathe. I feel him take my hand in his and squeeze, but I don't return the gesture.

People move around us as he leads me away. It's as though I'm watching this scene play out from a distance.

"We're leaving." I barely register Anthony's words as he

leads me away. What just happened? *Until you kill her.* No. I shake my head. No, it's not true. But he said it with such conviction. And didn't I always think he would? Didn't I know this would happen? *I should have run.* A small voice whispers inside of me. *Weak, you're so fucking weak.*

"You said they didn't know." I barely speak the words as Anthony leads me to the car. I have to keep blinking to focus. I feel lost and confused. That didn't just happen. It couldn't have. Everything was perfect. It was perfect. *It was fake.*

"Vince was the only one." *Was.* But now they all know.

I remember the look in Vince's eyes and everything changes. My world tilts on its side and my vision blurs with my tears. Vince isn't a forgiving man. He wants me dead, just like the Cassanos. I don't belong here. I watch Anthony as we drive away and the same cold, impassive look he had when I first *met* him is on his face.

In this moment I don't know why Anthony brought me here, but I do know two things for certain. The first is that Anthony lied to me. And the only other thing I know is that the Valettis want me dead.

CHAPTER 27

ANTHONY

"You're going to kill me?" she whispers as I shut the front door behind me. She walks aimlessly in the hall.

"No," I tell her again. She said it in the car and I shut that shit down. But she won't look at me. She doesn't believe me.

"I don't understand. Why?" She still doesn't look at me, and I hate it. What we had was pure. But now it's tainted with doubt.

"I've told you repeatedly I won't hurt you." She finally looks at me, but I can tell she doesn't believe me.

"Come here, kitten," I hold out my arms for her. She just needs my touch. I'll keep her safe. Vince can go fuck himself. They all can. I'll run away with her if I have to.

She looks at me, but takes a step back.

"I said come here." I take a step forward and she turns her back on me to run. She's defying me. She's running from me. It only takes three strides until my arms are wrapped around her small body and she's shrieking for me to let her go.

It hurts. It fucking kills me.

I walk to the basement with her struggling in my arms. She flails and kicks. She yells and cusses as I take her down the stairs. I almost drop her as I enter in the code. She's fighting me. She hates me. I know she does. My heart hurts, but I ignore it. I hold on to the anger. I hate that she thinks I'm lying to her. I've done nothing but tell her the truth. I will take care of her. She needs to calm down and listen. She has to listen to me.

I open the door to her cell and she looks up at me with anger and then betrayal in her large brown eyes. She needs to learn she can never question me. She'll learn.

She shakes her head and backs away from me as I stand in the doorway. Her body language and the look in her eyes make my heart squeeze with pain.

"You *will* obey me." I say the words with force, but they're choked. She looks back with defiance in her eyes. I don't recognize her, and she doesn't recognize me.

What we had is gone and I wish I could take it back. I hate Vince. I hate myself.

I watch in the monitor as she huddles into a ball on the concrete floor. Hard sobs rock through her small body, making her look weak and fragile. I know she's not at all weak. But she's become reliant on my approval and I know this hurts her.

I've seen this before. I've only had two subs before who thought they'd enjoy a complete power exchange.

They think they want to be told what to do. And they think they'll be able to listen, and be rewarded and pampered. But there always comes a time when the desire to obey is challenged too far. The desire can be lost over some concept of degradation or pride, or an issued command can simply be too far outside their comfort zone. Submissives have to learn to trust that everything their dom does is for their benefit. Doubt and lack of trust are the real issues.

Susan and Cassie were sweet girls. But when it came time to push them, it ended up like this. It would have never worked with them anyway. They cried and then left me. The only difference here is that Catherine can't leave me. Instead she'll hate me.

She doesn't trust me. I pace my room, not knowing what to do. I can't leave her in there to think about leaving me. Her cries ring out from the monitors and I walk quickly to turn them off. I can't take it.

It's my fault. It's all my fault. I don't think about anything other than what I want. And right now I want to comfort her.

I want her in my bed. I need her in my arms. I take the stairs two at a time until I'm at her door. No more locks. She'll learn to trust me. I'll do anything I can to prove it to her. She just needs to stay with me.

Stay with me.

I walk into the room with purpose, but she doesn't lift her head. I scoop up her body into my arms and hold her to my chest. I rock her gently and pet her back and her hair. Just holding her calms the beast pacing within me. She needs me, and I need her. That's all that matters. Doesn't she know that? She's all I need. I kiss her hair, but she doesn't look up. I walk us slowly to my room, but I don't even know if she notices.

I try to kiss her, but she shoves me away. I hold her closer to me, but she tells me, "No." She won't let me in. I watch her deny me over and over as she sheds her pain in my arms.

I want to make love to her and show her what she means to me. But I feel like I've already lost her. My need to control her was wrong. I shouldn't have punished her. It's my fault. I hold her close to me as she cries herself to sleep.

"I'm sorry," I whisper into her ear as her shoulders gently shake. "Please forgive me." She doesn't respond and I don't know if it's because she never will, or if she's fallen asleep.

I hold onto her as tight as I can and watch her. That security I've had since I first laid eyes on her is gone. I look down and I know I've lost her.

I shake my head and swallow the lump in my throat. I

don't know if I can make this right. I don't see how it's possible to move forward. I've broken her trust. I need her to forgive me, but I know she won't.

Chapter 28

Catherine

I can hear his steady heartbeat and feel his warm body against my back. We fit together perfectly, and that very thought frightens me to the core. My heart hurts as I try to ignore it. But this isn't right. I'm not okay. I'm falling in love with a man who's taken me against my will. These feelings can't be real. I need to leave. I have to get the fuck out of here before I lose what little sanity of I have left. Before he kills me.

I slowly move away from him and hate myself. I watch him sleeping peacefully and I have to cover my mouth to keep the sob from coming up and waking him. If I don't leave now, I may never have another chance. And I know I have to leave.

I walk as quickly and quietly as I can. I remember him

leaving the keys in the dining room. I know it's a risk trying to leave. He could come down here. He could take me back upstairs by force, or he could lock me away in the cell, and part of me hopes he does. I'm sick for having these thoughts, and I know it. But I use the knowledge that his *familia* won't keep me safe to motivate me. I summon my strength and force my limbs to move and go to the door. I take one last look around, gripping the frame and try to keep down the sickness threatening to come up.

I can't even take anything with me, because it's all locked in a room I don't have a code for. If that's not a fucking sign that this was never real, I don't know what is.

Rain beats against my skin and thin clothes as I run to the car. My heart pangs sporadically and I don't know if it's from the pain or the fear.

What hurts the most is knowing I would have stayed. I never would have questioned him. What we had was fucked up. But it was my fucked up fairytale come true. I loved him. I know I still do.

Tears cloud my vision and I brush them away, shoving the keys into the ignition. I look over my shoulder and hate the pain growing in my chest. I'm leaving him. I don't want to, but a small part of me is saying if I don't leave him now, I never will. Is it so wrong? I can't answer the question. "Forgive me," I whisper as I put the car in reverse and turn the wheel.

I don't care if it's wrong, I fucking loved him. Even

knowing he was going to kill me, I still love him and all his broken pieces.

I wipe the bastard tears from my eyes and sniffle as I speed away. I've left him. He's the only man I've ever truly loved, and I've left him. The car swerves and I fight the steering wheel in the rain to stay on the road. I try to steady my breath as a pain radiates in my chest.

In two turns, I'm out of the development and onto the busy road. It's late. It's nearly deserted, with just three cars parked at the front of the entrance.

I had to go, didn't I? I'm not safe with him. I shake my head in denial. He'd keep me safe, but he'd have to fight the world to keep me. I feel so torn and so confused. I hit the brakes and turn off the side of the road. I let the tears consume me.

I know I need to keep going. I need to run as fast as I can. He's going to find me if I stay here. The thought brings me more comfort than anything else. Maybe I'm sick. Maybe the feelings I have aren't healthy. But I hold on to them so I can calm myself. As I look in my rear-view mirror I spot the three cars from earlier driving toward me. None of the cars have their headlights on.

Something triggers inside of me and I quickly put the car into drive and hit the gas. As I speed up, so do they.

My heart beats in my chest with a fear I haven't felt in so long. They've found me. I swallow thickly and search the cars for a face. I don't know if it's the Valettis or the Cassanos, but as I make a sharp right and see them follow me, I know it's one or the other. I wish I could turn around and drive back to him. To Anthony. I wish he were here. I wish he could save me.

He would save me.

Out of instinct, I yell for Anthony. Tears fall down my face. No! I hit the gas harder and the back end of the car swerves. I try to straighten the wheel as my hands grip the leather and I pull to the right, but the car spins out, and in a blur my body smashes to the side. My head smacks against the wheel and my body falls limp. My hand touches my forehead and I look down at my fingers only to see blood. My vision spins and my breath feels hollow, but I have to run. I unbuckle the seatbelt and prepare to run. I have to run. I have to fight.

As my hand grips the handle, the door opens and I look up to see a sick smile from the last person I ever want to see.

"My little mouse came back to me." I hear his words, followed by the smash of his fist against the side of my temple. I'm vaguely aware that he's gripping my hair and pulling me out of the car, but I can't move my legs. Slowly, darkness overwhelms me, and I lose the battle to stay awake.

CHAPTER 29

ANTHONY

I push the curtain back and watch her drive away. I see her look over her shoulder with one last glance at the house, and it kills me not to run out and get her. I couldn't move as I felt her stir next to me and leave me. I knew that's what she was doing, and it took all of me to lie still and let her go free.

I knew she'd leave me. I was a fool to think I could have her. I was wrong to think she'd be safe with me.

She needs to leave me. I can't protect her. I need to let her go. She doesn't love me, and Vince will never let me keep her if she doesn't love me back.

They'll never understand.

If I could tell her anything right now, I'd tell her to run.

Run far away from me.

It hurts. The pain in my chest hurts so fucking much as I watch the car disappear.

She left me. I really thought it was love in her eyes.

Mom. I thought she loved me too.

When Dad killed her in front of me to get rid of the fear and the nightmares, she cried out how much she loved me. I thought that was love, too.

Maybe I'm wrong and I just don't know what love is.

If love is what's causing this pain, I don't want it. But I still want her. Fuck me, I do. I want to lie to myself and think that we can be together in this fucked up way and that the world will leave us alone. But I can't put her in danger. I've been selfish and stupid, and I fucking hate that I ever took her the way I did. At the same time, she's all I want. If I could go back upstairs and keep her lying in bed with me, I would. If I had to lock her up and never let her out again, I would. That's only more reason that I need to stay here and let her go. She deserves so much more than a man like me.

I sit outside in the rain, letting it soak through my clothes, just thinking about how I should have let her go right from the start. I should have let her go free. I thought I made her happy though. I thought she wanted the same things I wanted. But I was wrong.

I hear a car swerve in the distance and my heart starts pounding in my chest. I run inside for the keys to my pickup truck and haul ass as fast as I can. It can't be her. I pray she's okay. It takes too fucking long to get there. I'll save her. She needs me. I'll protect her. I slow the car as I see skid marks, but there's nothing there. It looks like a car crashed, but then drove off.

I stay at the scene for a long time, thinking it wasn't her. It wasn't my kitten.

She's left me and now she's safe. She's better off without me. I wish I had a way to track her to know for sure. Again, another reason she needs to run from me.

The pain won't go away.

I can't get rid of this hurt in my chest. I just know something's wrong.

I close my eyes and shake my head. It's all in my head. I'm only hurting because she left me. I'm looking for reasons to search her out. It's my own sickness.

I need to let her go. I settle on that truth as I drive back home. But I can't sleep. When the sun filters through the curtains and my phone pings a few hours later, I reach for it like it was meant to go off.

I expect it to be my kitten. I don't know how, but I do. All night I've waited up, hoping she'd come back to me.

I stare at the phone and I fucking hate myself. I click it off and move as quick as I can.

Cassys want a meet.

I know why. And I'm ready to end this. They're all fucking dead.

CHAPTER 30

ANTHONY

I can't stop pacing. It's not a fucking coincidence that the night she left we got a call for this meetup. We're supposed to meet at the garage in an hour. It's not right. Something's horribly wrong. She's not okay. I can feel it. My girl's not okay.

"Vince, it can't just be us two," I say. I know this is a setup. It's not just going to be Marcus there wanting to clarify the situation. There's more to this, and I know it deep down in my gut. He texted Vince to come meet with him, and later asked to bring me along. But I know this is a trap. I fucking know it.

"We can't trust them," I tell him again.

"What the fuck, Anthony?" Tommy asks me for the fourth fucking time.

I just shake my head. "It's not good. It's not going to be good."

Vince has been watching me like a fucking hawk. I haven't told him yet.

We're all here and I haven't said shit, but I can't shake this feeling. I need to tell them.

"Let me go in first," I finally speak up and look back at Vince. He doesn't answer.

"You're freaking me out, Anthony," Tommy says, grabbing my arm.

"You couldn't fucking listen!" Vince yells out, and it gets the attention of everyone. The air is thick with tension.

"You know I wasn't going to." I can't reach his eyes. I know I fucked up, but I need him right now. I can't let them hurt her. Not her. She didn't do anything wrong. She can't pay for my sins.

"What the fuck is going on?" Tommy asks with a pain that breaks through his words. He's worried. He's worried for me and it's all my fault.

"They have her; I know it." I say just above a whisper.

"Catherine?" Tommy asks, confused. It breaks my heart to know I've betrayed him. I betrayed all of them.

"Why? Why would they do that?" Tommy asks.

"War. It's the start of war." I answer him with pain in my chest.

"What'd you do?" Tommy demands to know as he shakes my shoulders, and I have to look him in the eyes, but I still can't tell him.

"Catherine's a rat. She's supposed to be dead." Vince answers over my shoulder and Tommy's grip loosens until his arms fall to his side. He looks at me like it can't be true. But it is.

"She had no choice." I try to defend her. They have to believe her; they have to believe me. She needs me. *She's mine.*

"This is over Catherine?" Tommy asks with doubt.

"She's mine," I say with finality. A look of hurt flashes in my brother's eyes. He doesn't understand. They'll never understand.

"You fucking bought her as a slave--" I understand Vince's anger, but I don't need it right now. I need him on my side. I need my *familia* to help me get her back. I need her. I need her right fucking now.

"I don't care if you don't understand. None of you ever understand me. That doesn't make me any less family. If I say she's mine, then she's fucking mine," I growl out.

"If she's yours, then how did they get her?" Vince steps up to me like he knows. Like he already knows that she left me. But that makes no difference to me. I let her go because I love her, and I'll save her because I love her. Even if she doesn't love me back.

"She left me."

Tommy grips his hair like he can't believe this shit. I hear the men walking around us, waiting on their orders, even though they already made up their minds. No one fucks with us. They mess with one of us, they fuck with all of us.

The only thing that would hold them back is if Vince told them not to.

"You didn't let her go?" Vince asks with disbelief.

"I watched her leave me. She needed to." I swallow the lump in my throat as I add, "But I know they have her. I know they found her." He looks at me with doubt and then nods slightly.

Vince looks past me and addresses the *familia.* "It doesn't matter what started it. Get your guns ready, boys, and call for the rest of 'em." I nod my head. Thank fuck. Thank fuck I have a real chance to save her, if they didn't already kill her.

"Anthony," Vince says to get my attention. I look up at him. We're going in first." I put my hand on his shoulder before he has a chance to move away. I lean in and give him a quick hug. He's shocked, and it takes him a moment, but he pats me on the back in return.

I don't let him go. "I have to save her, Vince." I pull back to look him in the eyes. "She can't die. I can't let her die." His brow furrows with confusion and I know I'm not getting through to him. He doesn't have to understand. He just has to give me his word.

"Don't be stupid--" he starts to answer me, but I cut him off.

"If it's between the two of us, save her. I can't let her die," I say.

That's the moment his look changes.

He gives me a small nod, and only then do I release him.

There she is. Just like I fucking knew she'd be. Fuck! She couldn't run fast enough, could she? It's my fault. She's on her knees with that fucker's hand gripping her shoulder, pushing her down. She looks up at me with the saddest expression and cries out, "I'm so sorry." The man behind her whips his hand across her face and she lands on her side. My hands fist at my side and my blood boils.

Not her. He's not going to get away with it. He cocks the gun in his hand and aims it at her head. His eyes are on me though.

"Was this little bitch worth it, Anthony? Was she worth war?" I hear the words but I can't take my eyes off of her. Lorenzo is still standing behind her. And behind him are a dozen or so of his men. I know I've walked into a sentencing. Her sentencing.

"Knock it off, Lorenzo." Marcus finally speaks. He puts his hands out as if to welcome us.

"What's this?" Vince asks from behind me as he walks up to my side. It's just the two of us, for now. "It was just supposed to be us, Marcus."

Marcus gives him a twisted smirk and shrugs his shoulder as he says, "Thought I might need a few more men to make my message clear."

Vince looks at Catherine and motions to her. "Is this really necessary?" He's keeping his voice even. If you didn't know him, you'd think he was completely unaffected. But I know him, and he's fucking pissed.

"It's the fucking rat your boy didn't fucking kill like he was supposed to."

"You know that's not what the deal was," Vince says as though he's on my side, but I know he's not. All this is my fault. I brought this onto my *familia*. I put us all in danger for her. Simply because I wanted her. I wanted to break something so beautiful. And I did. And now I have to take my punishment. I hope I fucking die today. I'll never forgive myself if I see her die though. I've watched death all around me my entire life, and it's never affected me. Not since my mother. But I can't today. Not her. Not my Catherine.

I walk toward the men and a few take a step back, but Marcus and Lorenzo hold their ground. "I bought her fair and square." I say the words like I'm not ready to rip them apart. Like this isn't war. Like this is just a business meeting over terms.

I hear the rest of my *familia* walk in behind us. A few guns cock. The clicks fill the air. Marcus' eyes turn hard. He tried to set us up, but the dumb fuck wasn't ready for an even match. The doors behind the Cassanos open and more of our crew walk in, guns loaded and ready. We have on our vests; I'm sure the Cassanos do as well, but this is nowhere near an even match. They're fucking dead.

"You really wanna do this, Vince?" Marcus sneers at my boss behind me. My eyes are locked on Lorenzo's. My hand's on my gun.

"You brought this on yourself. You wanted to put on a show," Vince says as he reaches for his gun, but keeps it pointed at the ground.

"What'd you think was gonna happen?" he asks. Silence fills the air and the men line up on both sides. We're in the middle. Vince is by my side, and my kitten on the floor just a few feet away from me. Everyone's armed but her. My eyes dart to hers and I can see she's already accepted it. She's gonna be the first to die.

I can't let it happen. I can't.

A few men start moving around. They're lining up. Some of the Cassanos start looking behind them, but most are going to be gunning for us. It doesn't matter either way, they're all going to die. The only thing they can do is try to take out a few of us first. I can't let that happen. I have to do something. She can't die, and our men can't go down because of my mistakes.

"Give her back, and we'll go away." I say the words and hate the weakness in my voice. I also hate that Vince is looking at me like I've lost my damn mind. He's ready for a fight. No one takes us on like this and makes fools of us. I know he won't stand for it. But I have to try. I'd beg them for her. I'd trade places with her if I could.

"It's not happening, Anthony. Not after you betrayed us." Marcus' voice rings out with clarity. He's firm in his decision.

"Take me instead then. Take me and it's over." Vince still hasn't said anything. I hear Tommy yell out from behind me. But Vince holds up his hand and silences him.

"Your gun," Marcus says loud enough for everyone to hear. I don't hesitate to lower myself, place my gun on the ground, and kick it away.

As I stand up, the fucking prick in front of me, Lorenzo, shrugs his shoulders and raises his gun at me. Every man in the room raises their weapon but me. I'll make the trade. I'll do it for her.

Catherine looks up with wide eyes and shakes her head. As the reality presses down on her, she does the stupidest fucking thing I can think of. She jolts upright and grabs the gun. She yanks it out of Lorenzo's hand. It falls to the floor with a loud clack and goes off. The room fills with the sounds of bullets.

"Fucking bitch," Lorenzo yells out and reaches for the gun. A bullet flies past me, but my eyes are on his gun. He's going to get it first. I see it happening in slow motion. I run to her and cover her small body as the sounds of bullets firing and men yelling ring out and ricochet off the wall.

She screams and cries. She tries to push away from me to fight. But I can't move, or she'll be in danger. She'll die. I have to protect her. I can't let her die. *Not her.* If I do anything good with my life, it'll be keeping her safe and alive. I need to get her through this. Even if I die, at least she'll know what I felt for her.

My body flinches with impact of a bullet, this one at close range. I feel a radiating pain throughout my shoulder as the bullet comes out the other side. The vest can only cover so much. I duck my head and tell her to stay down. I hear her crying and the thud of bodies hitting the floor. I lift my head for only a moment to look into her eyes and she looks wretched with guilt. I push my lips to hers to try to take the pain away. And as another bullet rips into my back, I do everything I can not to let her know.

I just want one more moment with her. One real moment where she can see the real me and what we really had.

The pain expands inside of me. I've been shot before, and more than once, but fuck it hurts. My body loses its strength and I fall onto her body, unable to brace myself any longer. I hear a few more shots and then silence. I don't look. I can't move. I can't risk her. It hurts. Fuck, it hurts. I cough and blood spills from my mouth. Men yell, "Take those three." Fists are smashing against flesh. I recognize the voices. We won. It's over.

"Anthony!" Vince calls out.

"Anthony," she cries out. Her grip on me is strong. She's okay. She's safe.

Vince pulls my body off of her and I lie flat on the ground. A pounding ache in my chest makes it hard to breathe.

"Anthony," she says as she holds on to me as she frantically searches my chest for the wounds. She's okay. She's on her knees, hovering over my body. Tommy comes up behind her.

"Take her away!" Vince yells.

I use the last of my strength and grip onto his shirt, pulling him close to me.

"Promise me she'll be safe, Vince." I hold his stare and make him promise me. "Promise me."

"I swear on my life, Anthony. But I don't need to tell you shit." He's bullshitting me. I know he is. Blood fills my mouth and it's hard to breathe. I should've died a long time ago. It's alright with me, as long as she's safe.

"You're gonna be fine. You'll make it through this," he says. I shake my head and let my head fall back.

"I love her, Vince. I don't deserve her, but I love her." I have to tell him. He has to believe me and take care of her when I'm gone.

"You can tell her yourself." Vince looks down at me as my vision starts to spin and darkness fades. "I promise I'll keep her safe for you."

The last words I hear come from her mouth as she pushes Tommy away and runs for me. "Anthony," she cries out. But I can't answer her. My world fades and I dream of her touch. Of her love.

CHAPTER 31

CATHERINE

"N o!" I scream while shaking my head in denial. They try to pry me away from Anthony. My hands grip onto his shoulders and my tears fall onto his chest. I feel numb everywhere, but my heart is aching.

Blood's soaks into Anthony's shirt and pools around his back as he lies still on the ground. "Help him!" I frantically scream out. They need to do something. He can't die. No! He can't leave me like this. He can't die because of me. *Please, God, save him.* I pray as I watch Vince rip off his shirt. Anthony doesn't move. His limp body sways as Vince looks over the bullet wound in his back.

I vaguely hear the grunting of men as they haul off dead

and limp bodies. I hear the smash of a fist pounding into tender flesh and threats being made. They took prisoners, but most of the men are surrounding their own man, the only Valetti to fall. My Anthony.

"Get her out of here," Vince yells back. He looks directly past my shoulder at Tommy who's holding me back.

"I can't leave him," I say. I search for understanding in Tommy's eyes, but he's not looking at me. He looks like he's carrying the pain that Anthony must be feeling. His eyes are full of anguish. He grips me closer to him as I try to push away and go back to Anthony. I can't let him die. He can't die.

"Right now you need to," Vince says as he looks at me, but it's not said with hate or anything other than sympathy.

"The cops are going to come and you can't be here. You shouldn't be anywhere around them." He motions to our left, where the Cassanos are all lined up execution style. My heart twists. I don't care about them. I don't care about any of this.

"I can't leave him," I cry out to Vince as Tommy drags me back.

"I won't tell you again." Vince looks me dead in the eyes. "If you never want to see him again, go ahead and stay. Have him try to explain it to the cops."

"You can't stay. Just listen to Vince. He'll take care of Anthony," Tommy whispers into my ear. I know he's hurting, too. I turn around in his arms and close my eyes tight, willing Anthony to be alright.

From my left, I hear a grunt of a laugh and someone spit. My eyes open and I see that prick. The bastard who started all of this. His hands are tied behind his back and he's on his knees. He's lined up like the others. Two of them are getting the shit beat out of them. But not Lorenzo. He looks at me with one black eye and gives me a bloody smile, and I've never wanted to hurt him more. I've never felt such a strong need for vengeance. It's his fault. All of this is his fault.

I don't think about it, and I don't consider the consequences. I just reach for Tommy's gun tucked in his waistband.

I hear his scream as I pull out of his grasp for just enough time to pull the trigger. I fire once, and it hits the fucker in his shoulder. I take a single step and scream with all the rage and pain I'm feeling. He falls backward with a cuss ringing in my ears. My second shot hits him square in the chest. Tommy's arms wrap around mine. Several men yell. I don't care. I stare at the man who made my life hell. The man who laughed at my pain. And I watch the life leave his eyes.

A strong hand rips the gun from my hand and I look up to see Vince scowling at me. He looks between me and Lorenzo. I can't look him in the eyes. I swallow the lump in my throat and stop fighting against Tommy. His hold on me loosens, and I instinctively try to go to Anthony. But Vince is blocking me, and Tommy's still gripping my wrist.

"Your ex?" Vince asks.

I nod my head as tears fall down my cheeks. I look back at

him. That piece of shit should have died long ago.

"You snitched 'cause of him?" he asks me. I fucking hate that he brings it up. I want to cower, but I don't. I nod my head in response. Vince looks me in the eyes and gives me a small smile as he says, "He fucking had it coming." He pats my shoulder and leans into my ear as he reassures me, "You did good."

He pulls away from me and I feel the faintest bit of relief. But it's not okay. Nothing can change what's happened. Lorenzo being gone won't bring Anthony back. He can't die on me.

"But don't do that shit again," Vince says to me, handing Tommy back his gun. "Get your shit together, Tommy."

"Let's go," Tommy says, pulling me away from the scene.

I hear someone ask Vince a question. I don't know what the question was, but I hear Vince's response clear as day.

"All of them. They're fucking done." Bullets ring out in an instant. I look over my shoulder to see the Cassanos falling to the ground, blood splattered on the ground in front of them. I should feel a sense of shock. But I feel nothing. I turn back around and let Tommy take me away before I give in to the urge to run back to Anthony.

I walk, but not by my own free will. I keep looking back, but they're surrounding Anthony. I can't see him. It hurts. It hurts too much. I feel like I'm dying. I get in the car, but I don't know how. All I can see is the look in Anthony's eyes as the bullets hit his back. I cover my face with my hands and let all the pain out as I sob.

"Catherine?" Tommy asks me after a long time. I look up and see that we're driving, but I don't know where we're going. He pulls over and holds me against him as I cry. His hand rubs gently on my back and for a moment I pretend it's Anthony. I pretend it's okay. "I know Anthony has problems. It's not his fault." He chokes on his words and refuses to look me in the eyes, "I'm sorry." I don't know how to respond, so I say nothing.

"Did he hurt you?" I hear the pain in Tommy's question and I look up at him with confusion. Did *Anthony* hurt me? It takes me a long time to gather the strength to answer. "No. Never." My heart twists with a pain I've never felt before.

"I didn't know he was keeping you against your will. I'm sorry," he whispers. "I'll take you anywhere you want, Catherine. You'll be safe. I'll make sure of it. He'll never find you if you don't want him to."

I shake my head frantically. "You don't understand. It's not like that. I want to go to Anthony," I insist. I hold onto Tommy's arm with an unrelenting grasp. My heart stammers in my chest and anxiety races through my blood. They can't send me away. I need to know he's okay.

"Do you love him?" Tommy asks.

"I do; I don't care if it's wrong." It's the truth, and I pray Tommy knows that. But he doesn't respond.

"He can't die for me; tell me he'll be okay." He has to be okay.

"I wish you'd ask me for something I can give you, Catherine, but I can't give you that."

CHAPTER 32

CATHERINE

The faint humming of the machines and the steady beeping of the monitors are the only sounds in the room, but I need to keep hearing them. They tell me he's alive. They removed the breathing tube from his throat today. It's been three days and they keep telling me he's going to wake up soon since now he can breathe on his own. They're just waiting on him now.

I'm waiting on him, too.

Tommy comes back into the room and hands me a styrofoam cup with a lid on it and the string from the teabag draped over the side. I give him a small smile and say thank you. I haven't slept at all. I didn't realize I haven't had to drink my tea or take my pills to sleep until I found myself curled up in the hospital chair, wide-awake and watching Anthony.

My voice is hoarse as I thank him.

"You can go if you want," Vince says from across the room as Tommy sags in the seat next to him. He keeps telling me that, and I give him the same response I did last time.

"I want to stay." He nods his head and looks down at his phone then back up at Tommy. They start talking in hushed tones. I don't mind. I don't listen. I just keep my eyes on Anthony's chest as it slowly rises and falls.

I put my cup down and scoot my chair closer to Anthony's bed. The clink of the metal is the only sound in the room. I take his hand in mine and rub my thumb along the palm of his hand and wait. I need him to hold me back. I just need a sign that he'll be alright.

I look up and my heart stops beating as Anthony clears his throat and his head turns to the side. He's waking up. My eyes widen and I do what I've been trained to do. I get onto my knees in the chair and kneel as best as I can. I watch my dom, my master, my love, and my life as I wait for him to wake and acknowledge me.

I see Vincent and Anthony rise from their seats from my periphery. I don't look at them though. I don't care what they think. I need Anthony to see me waiting for him like this. I need him to know I was waiting for him, that I would always be here for him.

His eyes slowly open and he looks down at me with confusion as he takes in a heavy breath and winces. My heart hurts for him. I know he's in pain.

"Kitten," he barely manages to get out.

"Anthony," I say as I look up at him and move my hands to his bed, crawling to get close to him.

"Can I get in with you?" I ask him. I know he's in pain, but I need to feel him. I need to be next to him and be by his side.

"Please," I beg him. "I need to feel you." He gives me a nod and watches as I quickly move to him. I never want to leave his side again.

I climb onto the small bed and hold him close to me. Tommy and Vince stand and talk to Anthony, but I don't listen. I can't do anything but hold him.

Once they're quiet I finally speak.

"I'm so sorry, Anthony," I say as I bury my head into his chest.

"Nothing to be sorry about." He kisses my hair and rubs my back. He's consoling me when he's the one who's so badly hurt. I pull away and brush the tears from my eyes while I shake my head.

"I never should've left you." I push down the sob threatening to choke me.

I look over to the left and see Vince and Tommy watching us. Both look confused and are obviously judging us, but I don't care. I need him to know how much I want him, how much I need him. I can't go back to a life without him. Never.

"I'll go to the cell. I deserve to be punished." I speak clearly and I know the other men heard, but I don't care if they know. It's none of their fucking business, and what they think of me is none of my business. I've never felt more safe and complete as I do with Anthony. I'm not letting that go.

"No, you need to go. Now," Anthony says dully as he stares at the back wall.

"You're throwing me away?" I ask him as my heart shatters in my chest. I shake my head in complete denial. I feel so broken. Every part of me hurts all the way to my soul.

"Please, Anthony," I beg him. "Please don't throw me away."

He closes his eyes and refuses to look at me. "You don't understand, Catherine. You're free now. No one will come for you. You can live your life in peace."

"We'll make sure you're safe and settled in." Vince interrupts us and motions for Tommy to follow him. He holds the door open and they both look back at us. "Whatever you two decide, we'll make sure you're safe, Catherine." He locks eyes with Anthony for a moment before leaving and closing the door behind him.

"But I don't want to go." My shoulders shake and my voice cracks. I try to scoot closer to him and he lets me. Thank God he lets me. "Please, Anthony. I can't live without you."

"You can." His hand cups my chin and his thumb strokes against my jaw. I lean into his warmth and kiss his palm.

"You'll find a man who can love you." It breaks my heart that he's willing to let me go. That he's shoving me away. "I don't deserve you." He says the words with finality.

"Just the fact that you're saying that means you do." I breathe out the words, my hands clutching his. I need him to take me back.

"I'll do anything." I will. I'll do anything he wants for him to take me back.

"Then leave me," he says.

"I won't." I almost yell the words, but somehow, saying it in a calm voice and locking my eyes on his, it comes out with force.

His eyes heat with anger and a dark lust that I've missed. "Are you disobeying me, kitten?" he asks. His chest rises and falls with a sharp intake of air.

"Yes. I am." I stare back at him defiantly, hoping it's enough. That his need to punish me is enough that he'll keep me. Even if he doesn't realize it, I know he loves me. And I love him.

I close my eyes and gather up the courage to spill my truth to him. "I love you, Anthony." I wipe the tears away angrily. "You'd better not throw me out. I'd rather die."

"You wouldn't," he says as though he knows it to be true.

"I would. I can't live without you." The pain in my chest is unbearable. I know I won't be okay without him. Never.

"I did that to you," he says with regret.

"You did what I wanted, Anthony. You always did what

I wanted." I take his hand in mine and press his palm to my cheek. "I need you now more than I ever did. I'll beg until you cave. I swear I will."

He looks at me for a long time and I remain still, waiting for his verdict. My heart pumps slowly in my chest as though it's prepared to stop beating if he denies me.

"Come here, kitten." I crawl up to him, loving my pet name. I nestle into his side, careful not to hurt him. "You've been very disrespectful," he says, staring into my eyes. "And you disobeyed me. You left me, and then disobeyed me again. You put yourself in danger." His admonishment makes my shoulders droop in shame. What's worse is that it's all true.

"I'm sorry, Anthony."

"Don't be," he says, taking my chin in his hand and tracing my lower lip with his thumb. "If you come back to me now," he says, "I'll never let you go."

My heart swells in my chest and I push my lips to his. My tear-stained cheeks heat as he kisses me back with the passion I know he has for me. I break our kiss and finally breathe.

"Never let me go, Anthony." I look into his tortured eyes and I hurt so much for him. For everything he's been through, but also because I know leaving the way I did hurt him, and I fucking hate that. "I love you." I'll say it every day until he believes me, although I'm not sure he ever will.

His forehead scrunches and he takes in a deep breath. He swallows thickly and looks out of the hospital window.

Finally, he looks back to me and says the words I want to hear every day for the rest of my life. "I love you, too. But that's not even close enough to describing what I feel for you. I want you to remember that. Always."

CHAPTER 33

ANTHONY
Months Later

I've been looking for Catherine everywhere and I'm trying to push away the feeling that something's wrong. I keep waiting for her to leave me again, no matter how many times she says she loves me. She says I just need time to accept it, and maybe that's true. I don't care what holds us together, so long as she never leaves me.

I almost pass by the pile of two-by-fours and cans of paint, but then I catch sight of her out of the corner of my eye. She's curled up in a ball on the reading nook I built for her. Each wall is a shelf for her books and there's a giant window with a bench that I plan on padding for her. She's curled up on the wood, napping.

"I gave you a fitting pet name, kitten," I say as I pet her hair. She blinks a few times and yawns. She's been tired from the move and from all the changes, but the one thing that stays the same is the look of devotion I get from her every waking moment. The move's been good for her. She said she needed to be close to family. My *familia*. *Our familia*.

I have to admit it's been good for her. For me, too. Which is surprising. Even Vince seems to be as happy as a pig in shit. And Catherine and Elle are thick as thieves when it comes to planning these fucking get-togethers she forces me to attend. Apparently having a girl that gets along well with everyone looks good for me and makes me more approachable. I'm still on my own when it comes to work, but that's the way I want it.

I'm about to whip her ass though and she should know it. "You were supposed to be upstairs twenty minutes ago," I tell her with a hard voice. She knows it's play though. There's a time for that side of me to come out, and right now, it's time. She wanted to play, and so did I. She should've been there to greet me on her knees.

Her eyes go wide and she's quick to pick up her phone. She checks it and shakes her head as she taps the screen and looks at her alarms. She winces and holds the phone up for me to see. She never turned the alarm on.

"I really hate to have to do this," I say even though I fucking don't hate it at all. She looks up with a bit of apprehension, but her eyes are full of lust and her legs subconsciously fall open. She knows she's going to be cumming soon. She's a spoiled pet. But I fucking love it.

I sit next to her on the bench and she quickly sits up and waits.

Since moving I've punished her ass at least a dozen times. Not for disobeying me, since she knows better than that. She deliberately disobeyed me once before we moved. She sought out Vince after I told her not to. I told her to leave it alone and let us break off from the *familia*. I thought it was best, but she defied me. My hand twitches remembering how I spanked her. I got her on edge and left her there, alone and crying. She took her punishment and waited for me to go back to her. It couldn't have been more than fifteen minutes. I'm not a man who makes love to a woman, but if I ever have, it was with her that night. And then of course I gave her what she wanted.

"What's my punishment, Anthony?" she asks as she looks up at me with big doe eyes. She's an awful actress. There's nothing but excitement on her face.

"I set the bench up in the dungeon." I can't help but smile at her name for the basement. She bought a whip and a riding crop, stuck them in the corner on top of a bed and called it the dungeon. My little kitten is fucking adorable.

Her eyes glaze over with longing and she speaks in a breathy voice. "Yes, Anthony." She loves that bench. I had to reinforce it because I almost broke it the last time I fucked her on it.

My brow furrows as she waits for me to lead her to the basement so she can take her punishment.

"Do you still want to play, kitten?" I ask her. After everything we've been through, I keep thinking one day she won't want this. One day she'll decide she doesn't want this anymore.

"Always," she answers. "I'll always be your kitten, and you can be my bad boy." She tells me like it's a fact.

"Boy? No, kitten. I'm a bad man." It's the truth, and I wish she'd just accept it, but I don't think she ever will.

Her eyes go soft and fill with sadness.

"You aren't a bad man." She shakes her head and it breaks my heart. I wish I'd never burdened her with my shit. None of that matters; it's in the past where it belongs. And my sweet love is my future. It's all for her.

"Bad boy?" I ask her. She's gotta be fucking kidding me.

"It's a genre of romance," she explains.

Jesus Christ.

"Call me whatever you want, kitten, when we're home. But please don't call me your romantic bad boy in front of another human being ever." That has her eyes filling with laughter and a silent giggle shaking her shoulders. That's my girl.

I finger the ring in my pocket nervously. I just got it back from the jeweler. I had it custom designed for her to match her owl earrings. It took a little convincing, but now that she doesn't fear losing them, she never wears anything else. I thought rubies in her engagement ring would be a nice touch.

It's the entire reason I wanted to play today. I need her to do this for me. We need this.

"You know you love it," she teases me. As she says the words I slip the ring on her finger. She pulls back with a gasp and stares down at the diamond. She covers her mouth with her other hand.

"Marry me, Catherine." I tell her simply. I want everyone everywhere to instantly know she's mine. Always.

She nods her head as tears slip down her cheeks. She rises from her chair and wraps her arms around my neck as she says, "Yes, Anthony."

"I love you, Catherine," I whisper as I lean down for a kiss.

"I love you too, Anthony."

EPILOGUE

CATHERINE

I type away and continue hitting the keys even though I hear him coming. I just have to get this thought out before I forget. I was hit with a wave of inspiration for this scene and I don't want to lose it. I've been writing steadily ever since we moved into the new house. My office has a huge window, just like it did at our old place. Well, this one's even bigger, but the feeling is the same.

He walks up behind me at the back of my desk and rests his hands on my shoulders, but other than that, he doesn't interrupt. It only takes a minute for me to finish my thought and when I do, I'm quick to look up at him and give him a small smile. I reach my hand behind his neck and pull him down to me for a kiss.

"Mmm." He hums against my lips. "What is my naughty girl up to?" I blush at his low tone and rest my head against his chest.

"I wanted to write our story." I feel him stiffen behind me, but I keep going and decide to spill it all. "All of our stories."

"Kitten," Anthony says in an admonishing tone.

"No, no. It's fiction. Under a pen name. No one will ever know." I look up at him searching for approval. I love romance novels, and I just have to write all these love stories I've heard. The whole family is filled with fairytales, albeit dirty smutty fairytales, that have to be told. I've never felt compelled so much in my life to write them down. Ours will be last, because in my completely unbiased opinion, it's the best.

He smirks at me and places a hand on the nape of my neck, massaging slightly. "Can I read them?"

"If you want to." I wouldn't be shocked if he did. He reads over my work from time to time. I used to think he was making sure that I wasn't trying to put clues or hints out there for someone to come rescue me from him. *As if.* But then he started doing things in bed that were incredibly familiar from my blogs and columns.

"Well, I definitely want to read ours. I wanna know what my kitten was thinking when I brought her home." He smiles warmly at me with love in his eyes before leaning down to give me a sweet kiss. My chest warms with his affection.

"I have a question I need to know... for the story." I don't know what he'll answer. But I really do want to know. "Why didn't you have me call you master?" I ask him.

It takes him a moment to answer. "I knew from the second I saw you that I would be just as much a slave to you as you would ever be to me. If not more." Tears prick my eyes. I fucking love his answer. "Doesn't matter what you call me, babe," he says as he tips my chin up so I have to look at him, "You'll always be my kitten."

"You'll always be my *bad boy*." That earns me a chuckle as I lean into his chest savoring how happy we both are.

It might not be ideal or perfect, but I'm more than satisfied with my happily ever after.

About the Author

Thank you so much for reading my romances. I'm just a stay at home Mom and an avid reader turned Author and I couldn't be happier.

I hope you love my books as much as I do!

More by Willow Winters
www.willowwinterswrites.com/books

Made in the USA
Monee, IL
21 November 2023